"I'm pregnant."

Pregnant? What the h

Nash stared at Lily, kn
lying. After all, she loo
felt, and what would sh
him? She didn't know his identity, didn't know who
he truly was or how something like this would be
perfect blackmail material.

In Lily's eyes, and the eyes of everyone else on the
estate, he was a simple groom who kept to himself
and did his job. Little did they know the real reason
he'd landed at the Barrington's doorstep.

And a baby thrown into the mix?

Talk about irony and coming full circle.

* * *

Carrying the Lost Heir's Child
is part of The Barrington Trilogy:
Hollywood comes to horse country—and the
Barrington family's secrets are at the center of it all!

* * *

If you're on Twitter,
tell us what you think of Harlequin Desire!
#harlequindesire

Dear Reader,

If you've been following the Barrington family saga, you're familiar with the mysterious groom, Nash. I've never had a character speak to me in such a forceful, bold way before, but Nash really pushed his way from the back of my mind straight to the front...those alpha men. :-)

The irony of having Nash fall in love with beautiful Hollywood starlet Lily Beaumont threw me off track for a bit. As soon as the idea developed, I knew I had to run with it. Their story kept me up nearly every night as scene after scene played through my head faster than I could crank out the words. I'm so glad to end this series with this passionate couple who struggle to keep hold of the important things in life.

Nash and Lily may come from money, they may have any material possession within their reach, but they put family, loyalty and love above all else. Throw in an unexpected pregnancy and Lily and Nash truly have to fight for something they didn't even know they were searching for.

I hope you enjoy Nash's growth and Lily's strength as she encourages Nash in the most difficult time of his life. It takes a strong woman to be with a man like Nash, to put up with all the secrets...secrets that could destroy the family they're just starting.

I hope you've enjoyed the Barrington trilogy as much as I have!

Happy reading,

Jules

CARRYING THE
LOST HEIR'S CHILD

———

JULES BENNETT

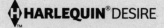

Recycling programs
for this product may
not exist in your area.

ISBN-13: 978-0-373-73365-1

Carrying the Lost Heir's Child

Printed in U.S.A.

HARLEQUIN®
www.Harlequin.com

National bestselling author **Jules Bennett**'s love of storytelling started when she would get in trouble as a child and would tell her parents her imaginary friends were to blame. Since then, her vivid imagination has taken her down a path she'd only dreamed of. And after twelve years of owning and working in salons, she hung up her shears to write full-time.

Jules doesn't just write Happily Ever After—she lives it. Married to her high school sweetheart, Jules and her hubby have two little girls who keep them smiling. She loves to hear from readers! Contact her at authorjules@gmail.com, visit her website, www.julesbennett.com, where you can sign up for her newsletter, or send her a letter at P.O. Box 396, Minford, OH 45653. You can also follow her on Twitter and join her Facebook fan page.

Books by Jules Bennett

Harlequin Desire

The Barrington Trilogy

When Opposites Attract...
Single Man Meets Single Mom
Carrying the Lost Heir's Child

Harlequin Special Edition

The St. Johns of Stonerock series

Dr. Daddy's Perfect Christmas

Visit Jules Bennett's profile page
at Harlequin.com for more titles.

To Gems for Jules—
the best street team an author could ask for!
You all are so amazing and supportive. I love you all!

One

The masculine aroma. The strength of those arms. The hard chest her cheek rested against…she'd know this man anywhere. She'd watched him across the grassy meadows, dreamed of him…made love to him.

Lily Beaumont struggled to wake and realized all too quickly she didn't have a clue how she'd gotten here.

Or more to the point, where was "here"?

The straw rustled against the concrete floor beneath her. She lay cradled in Nash James's lap, his strong arms around her midsection. What on earth had happened?

"Relax. You fainted."

That low, soothing voice washed over her. Lily lifted her lids to see Nash's bright blue eyes locked on hers. Those mesmerizing eyes surrounded by dark, thick lashes never failed to send a thrill shooting through her. No leading man she shared the screen with had ever been this breathtaking…or mysterious.

But, she'd fainted? She never fainted.

Oh, yeah. She'd been walking to the stables to talk to Nash…

"Oh, no." Lily grabbed her still-spinning head. Reality

slammed back into her mind, making her recall why she was in the stables. "This isn't happening."

Rough, callused fingertips slid away strands of hair that had fallen across her forehead. "Just lie still," he told her. "No rush. Everyone is gone for the day."

Meaning the cast and crew had all either gone to the hotel or into their on-site trailers. Thank God. The last thing she needed was a big fuss over her fainting spell, because then she'd have some explaining to do.

Just a few short months ago Lily started shooting a film depicting the life of Damon Barrington, dynamic horse owner and a force to be reckoned with. The Barrington estate had become her home away from home and the quiet, intriguing groom whose lap she currently lay in had quickly caught her attention.

Before she knew it, she'd been swept into a secret affair full of sneaking around, ripping off clothes and plucking straw pieces from her hair...which led her to this moment, this life-altering moment when she was about to drop a major bomb in Nash's life.

All the trouble they'd gone through to keep their escapades a secret were all in vain. No way could this news stay hidden.

"Nash." She reached up to cup his face, the prickle of his short beard beneath her palm a familiar sensation. "I'm sorry."

His brows drew together, worry etched across his handsome, tanned face, and he shook his head. "You can't help that you passed out. But you scared the life out of me."

Lily swallowed, staring at such an attractive, spellbinding man could make a woman forget everything around her... like the fact that she was carrying this man's child.

"Are you feeling okay?" he asked, studying her face. "Do you need something to eat?"

Just the thought of food had her gag reflex wanting to

kick in again. Weren't pregnant women supposed to be sick in the mornings? What was this all-day nonsense?

Lily started to sit up, but Nash placed a hand over her shoulder. "Hold on. Let me help you."

Gently, he eased her into a sitting position as he came to his feet. Then he lifted her, keeping her against his firm, strong body the entire time. Strong arms encircled her waist again and Lily wanted to seek the comfort and support he was offering. This might have been the first tender moment between them, considering anytime she'd come to meet him after dark they hurried to the loft where their passion completely took control.

How on earth would he react to the news? She was still reeling from the shocker herself, but she refused to keep this a secret. He had a right to know. She honestly had no clue what Nash would say, what he would do. A baby didn't necessarily affect his line of work. Hers, on the other hand…

She'd been burned so badly before and had fought hard to overcome the public scandal that ensued. How would he handle being thrust into the limelight?

Lily groaned. Once the story broke, the press would circle her like vultures—and they would make her private life a top headline. People were starving, homeless, fighting wars and the media opted to nose their way into celebrities' lives and feed that into homes around the world rather than something that was actually newsworthy.

Lily loved being an actress, loved the various characters she got to tap in to and uncover. But she hated the lack of privacy. A girl couldn't even buy toilet paper without being spotted. Lily prided herself on being professional, doing her job and doing it well, and staying out of the media's greedy, sometimes evil, clutches…a nearly impossible feat.

"You okay now?" he asked, his breath tickling the side of her face.

Nodding, Lily stepped away, immediately missing the warmth of his body, but thankful the dizziness had passed.

Over the past couple months she'd actually come to crave his touch, miss him when he wasn't near her. She should've known then she was getting in over her head where this virtual stranger was concerned. Their passion had swept her into a world she'd never experienced before. How could any single woman turn away from a man who touched her beneath the surface, who looked so deep within she was certain he could see in to her soul?

A physical connection was something she could handle. But all of those nights of sneaking around, of giving in to their desires had caught up with them. Now they would have to pivot away from the sex-only relationship and actually talk about the future…a future she'd never expected to have with this man.

With her back to him, Lily tried to conjure up the right words, the words that would soften the blow, but really was there a proper way to tell someone they were going to be a father? No matter how gentle the words were, the impact and end result would still be the same.

"Nash—"

Before she could finish her sentence, Nash took hold of her shoulder, eased her around and framed her face with his firm hands. Hypnotized by those vibrant blue eyes, she said nothing else as his mouth claimed hers.

And that right there was the crux of their relationship. Passion. Desire. Instant clothes falling to the floor.

Some might have said having a secret affair in the stables on a film set was not the classiest of moves, but Lily didn't care. She'd been classy her whole life…now she wanted to be naughty. The secret they shared made their covert encounters all the more thrilling.

Who knew Hollywood's "girl next door," as they'd dubbed her, had a wild side? Well, they'd caught a glimpse of it with the scandal, but she had since reclaimed her good girl status. She certainly had never been this passionate with or for a man. Definitely not the jerk who had used her and exploited her early in her career.

Before she'd become a recognized name, she'd fallen for another rookie actor. He'd completely blind-sided her by filming her without her knowledge. Their most intimate moments had been staged; everything about their relationship had been a lie. After that scandal, Lily had to fight to get to where she was now.

Nash's arms enveloped her and Lily was rendered defenseless as his mouth continued its assault on hers. Her arms slid up the front of his shirt, taut muscles firm beneath her palms.

He eased back slightly, resting his forehead against hers. "You sure you're feeling okay? Not dizzy anymore?"

"I'm okay," she assured him, clutching his T-shirt.

Nash's lips nipped at hers. "I missed you today. I kept seeing you and Max together. It was all I could do to ignore the way his arms were around you. His lips where mine should be."

Chills spread over her body. Tingles started low in her belly and coursed throughout. That hint of jealousy pouring from Nash's lips thrilled her more than it should…considering this was supposed to be a fling.

"We were acting," she murmured against his mouth. "You know we're playing a young couple in love."

Lily had wanted to play the role of the late Rose Barrington since news of the project had first spread, and having Max Ford as the leading man was perfect. She and Max had been friends for years…so much so that he was like a brother to her.

Nash's hands slid between them, started peeling down the top of her strapless sundress.

"If Max weren't married with a baby, I'd think he was trying to steal my time with you."

Baby. Just the word threw a dose of reality right smack-dab in the middle of their minor make-out session.

Lily covered Nash's hands with her own and eased back. "We need to talk."

Vibrant eyes stared back at her beneath heavy lids. "Sounds like you're breaking things off. I know we never discussed being exclusive." Nash attempted a smile. "Don't take my Max joke so seriously."

Shaking her head, Lily took a deep breath and pushed through her fear and doubts. "I didn't take you for the jealous type. Besides, I know what this is between us."

Or, what it had started out being.

"Oh, baby, I'm jealous." He jerked her against his body. "Now that I've had you, I don't like seeing another man's hands on you, but I know this is your job and I love watching you work."

"I can't think when your hands are on me," she told him, stepping back once again to try to put some distance between temptation and the truth.

A corner of Nash's devilish mouth kicked up. "You say that like it's a bad thing. Because I'm thinking plenty when my hands are on you."

Smoothing a hand through her hair, Lily tried to form the right words. Since seeing the two blue lines on the stick this morning and confirming what she'd already assumed, she'd been playing conversations on how to break the news over and over in her mind. But now it was literally show time and she had nothing but fear and bundles of nerves consuming her.

"Nash…"

Abandoning his joking, Nash's brows drew together as he reached for her once again. "What is it? If you're worried about when you leave, I don't expect anything from you."

"If only it were that easy," she whispered, looking down at his scuffed boots, inches from her pink polished toes.

Nash was a hard worker, so unlike the Hollywood playboys who always tried to capture her attention. Money and fame meant nothing to her—she had plenty of both. She preferred a man who worked hard, played hard and truly cared for other people…a man like Nash.

This wasn't supposed to happen. None of it. Not the deeper feelings, not the lingering looks that teetered on falling beyond lust and certainly not a baby that would bind them forever.

"Lily, just say it. It can't be that bad."

She met and held his questioning stare. "I'm pregnant."

Okay, maybe it *could* be that bad.

Pregnant? What the hell? Suddenly he felt like passing out himself.

Nash stared at Lily, knowing full well she wasn't lying. After all, she looked just as freaked out as he felt and what would she have to gain by lying to him? She didn't know his true identity, or how something like this would be perfect blackmail material.

In Lily's eyes, and the eyes of everyone else on the estate, he was a simple groom who kept to himself and did his job. Little did they know the real reason he'd landed at the Barringtons' doorstep.

And a baby thrown into the mix?

Talk about irony and coming full circle.

"You're positive?" he asked, knowing she wouldn't have told him had she not been sure.

Lily nodded, wrapping her arms around her middle and worrying her bottom lip. "I've had a suspicion for several days, but I confirmed this morning."

Well, this certainly put a speed bump in all the plans he had for his immediate future here at Stony Ridge Acres. Not to mention life in general. A baby wasn't something he was opposed to, just something he'd planned later down the road… after a wife came into the picture.

"I have no idea what to say," he told her, raking a hand through his hair that was way longer than he'd ever had. "I… damn, I wasn't expecting this."

Lily kept looking at him as if she was waiting for him to explode or deny the fact the baby was his. Of course, she could've slept with someone else, but considering that they'd been together almost every night for nearly the past two months, he highly doubted it.

Besides, Lily wasn't like that. He many not know much about her on a personal level, but he knew enough to know she wasn't a woman who slept around. Despite that whole sex scandal she'd endured years ago, Nash wasn't convinced she was some crazed nympho.

But he also wasn't naive and he wasn't just an average groom, so he needed to play this safe and protect himself from all angles.

"The baby is yours," she stated, as if she could sense where his thoughts were going. "I haven't been with anybody since months before I even came here."

"I thought you said you were on birth control."

"I am," she countered. "Nothing is foolproof, though. I'm assuming it happened that one time we…"

"Didn't use a condom."

One time in all those secret rendezvous he had thought he'd put one in his wallet, but they'd used it already. They'd quickly discussed how they were both clean, amidst clothes flying all over the loft floor, and they'd come to the mutual decision to go ahead… Thus the reason for this milestone, life-altering talk they were having now.

Emotions, scenarios, endless questions all swirled through his mind. What on earth did he know about babies or parenting? All he knew was how hard his mother worked to keep them in a meager apartment. She'd never once complained, never once acted worried. She was the most courageous, determined woman he'd ever known. Traits she'd passed down to him, which gave him the strength to carry on with his original plans, even with the shocking news of the baby. He would not let his child down, but he had to follow through and take what he had come for.

"I don't expect anything from you, Nash," Lily went on as if she couldn't handle the silence. "But I wasn't going to keep this a secret, either. Secrets always become exposed at the wrong time and I felt you deserved to know. It's up to you whether you want to be part of this baby's life."

Secrets, hidden babies. Wow. The irony kept getting harsher and harsher as if fate was laughing at him. This hurdle she'd placed in front of him really had him at a cross-roads. What started out as a fling had now escalated into something personal, intimate…anchoring him in for the long term. Because now he couldn't keep pretending to be some-one he wasn't, unfortunately he couldn't come clean with his identity, either.

He wanted to give his child, and Lily, the absolute best of everything. Even though Lily wasn't financially strained, Nash would be front and center in his child's life in every single way. How the hell could he do that without her dis-covering his identity?

Damn it. He'd never, ever intended for her to be hurt, but he'd passed the point of no return and now the inevitable heartbreak lay in the very near future.

She was never supposed to know who he really was. She was supposed to be gone well before he revealed himself. But now she would be part of his life forever and there was no escaping that hard fact.

"I would never leave you alone in this, Lily." He stepped forward, sliding his hands up over her smooth, bare shoul-ders. His thumbs caressed the edge of her jaw as an ache settled deep within him, knowing he would cause her even more pain. "How are you feeling? I assume the pregnancy is why you passed out?"

"I'm feeling okay. I've been very nauseous for several days, but this is the first time I've fainted." Her eyes sought his as a smile tugged at her unpainted lips. "I'm glad you were there to catch me."

"Me, too."

He still craved her, ached for her, even with the stunning news. Nash slid his mouth across hers, needing the contact and comfort that only she could provide. When he'd go back to his small rental cottage at night, he'd long for her even though he'd just been intimate with her. Nash had never been swept into such a fast, intense affair before.

And his attraction had nothing to do with her celebrity or her status as one of Hollywood's most beautiful leading ladies. Lily was genuine, not high maintenance or stuffy. Nash honestly admired her. The fact that she was sexy as hell and the best lover he'd ever had was just a bonus.

Her lips moved beneath his, her arms wrapped around his neck as her fingertips toyed with the ends of his hair. Even though they'd been secretly seeing each other for a couple of months, their passion had never once lessened. This woman was so responsive, so perfectly matched for him that he simply couldn't get enough.

Right now they had more pressing issues to deal with… not to mention the ones he had to face on his own.

Damn it. He'd wanted to keep her out of his own sordid affairs and keep things strictly physical. But now Lily discovering the truth about him was unavoidable. There was no way he could avoid the crushing blow that would eventually come down. He could delay the bombshell, weigh his options, because he didn't just have Lily and a baby to think about…he had another family to consider.

Stepping back, Nash studied her, processing just how vulnerable she was right at this moment and knew the end result of his lies would be the same. Once she figured out who he was, she would want nothing to do with him. There was no way in hell he'd be absent from his child's life, though, which meant Lily couldn't be rid of him no matter how much she would come to hate him.

"I'll walk you to your trailer so you can pack your things."

Lily jerked back. "Pack my things?"

"You're coming to stay with me."

Lily completely removed herself from his touch and crossed her arms over her chest. "Stay with you? Why on earth would I do that?"

"So I can take care of you."

Laughing, Lily shook her head. "I'm not dying, Nash. I'm having a baby."

"My baby," he corrected. "I want you with me, Lily."

"How am I going to explain why I'm living with you and not in my trailer? Nobody knows about our affair."

Nash shrugged. "I don't care what they think. I care about your health and our baby."

"Well I care," she all but shouted, throwing her hands to the side. "The media is just waiting to publish something juicy on me. Don't you understand that I have a career, a life, and I can't throw it away because you want to take charge? I've worked too hard to overcome the reputation Hollywood first gave me. I'm no longer the wild child of the industry. I'm respected and I'd like to keep it that way."

Fine, so he was thinking selfishly, but still, he refused to let her go through this alone. Just the thought of his mother being in this position once upon a time had his stomach tightening. Besides, this was Lily. She was a drug in his system and having her close by at all times would only feed their sexual appetite even further.

Maybe he needed to rein in the testosterone. But only for now and only because he refused to back down. He would still find a way to keep her close whether she liked it or not. Yes, he wanted the sex, but now that there was a child involved…he wanted to be right there every step of the way for his son or daughter.

"Fine. I'll come stay with you."

Lily raised a brow and tilted her head. "Seriously, Nash. I'm fine. I'm not going to do anything but sleep and work."

"That's what concerns me," he retorted. "You're getting tired and you're pushing yourself because the film is almost finished. You passed out, for crying out loud."

"I can't stop working."

Moments ago he'd been ready to take her up to the loft. Now he was struggling with how many more lies he would have to tell before this was all over.

Horses shifted in their stalls behind him, the sunset cast a bright orange glow straight through the wide-open stable doors. The setting epitomized calm and serenity...too bad the storm inside him was anything but.

"What about after you're done filming? What will we do about the baby?"

And there it was. The ultimate question that wedged heavily between them, but he had to throw it out there. He had to know what her plans were. He wasn't ready for a family by any means, but considering he and Lily lived on opposite sides of the country, they needed to figure out how they could both be in this child's life.

Lily smoothed her hair away from her face, turned away from him and sighed. "I don't know, Nash. I truly don't know."

They had time to consider how to deal with the baby. For now, Nash needed to stick with his original agenda and nothing could get in his way. He'd done enough spying, enough eavesdropping to calculate his next move.

He'd had many reasons—professional and personal—for taking on a new identity. But the main reason was the horses he needed from Damon. Those horses were the final pieces in the stable he'd spent years creating. He would move heaven and earth to get them.

As he watched Lily, her worried expression, her still-flat belly, Nash came to the realization that the truth he'd come here to disclose had nothing to do with Lily. Yet, because of a decades-old secret, Lily and his baby might pay the price.

All he had to do was figure out a way to get Damon to sell him the horses, go back to his own estate and keep his child in his life.

One monumental obstacle at a time.

Two

Well, she'd lost only part of the battle. She wasn't going back to Nash's place, but he was escorting her to her trailer. And she was almost positive he intended to spend the night.

A thrill shot through her, but would their cover be blown? He'd promised to be up and in the stables working before sunrise so he shouldn't be spotted. She didn't want him to think she was ashamed, far from it. Unfortunately, her reputation was always at stake and after the scandal from years ago, the press would love to see her "backslide" into bad girl mode. She refused to give them any fodder.

Nash knew of the sex video that had been leaked and he knew how sensitive she was about her privacy. Being a very private, secretive person himself only made their hidden affair the perfect setup. They'd been able to sneak around on the private grounds for months now.

Thankfully, the press wasn't on-site because of the security who kept them outside the gates. Still, she worried. What if a member of the crew spotted them together? What if they leaked a story? She couldn't endure another scandal, she just didn't have the energy to fight it, and she wouldn't put her mother through that again.

"Relax." Nash squeezed her hand. "Nobody can see us. It's dark."

He was right. Nobody was around, but she was used to being in the loft of the stables where she was sure no one would see or hear them. Right now, walking across the Barringtons' vast estate to head toward her on-site trailer, Lily just felt so exposed. Their footsteps were light and all was quiet except for an occasional frog croaking, a few crickets chirping and a horse neighing every now and then. They were utterly alone.

Before discovering the baby, Lily had wanted to talk to Nash about her feelings…feelings that had grown deeper than she'd expected. They'd both agreed that everything they shared was temporary and physical, but somewhere along the way her heart had gotten involved. She didn't want to open up now or he'd probably think she was just trying to get a husband to go along with the baby to keep the gossip at bay.

With Nash's rough fingers laced through hers, Lily had to admit she loved the Neanderthal routine when he'd gone all super protective of her. She'd known from the moment she met Nash that he was a man of power, of authority.

Her stepfather had been a man of power, too, waving his money around to get what he wanted. Nash was different, though. He was type A, without all the material possessions. He appealed to her on so many levels; she just wished they weren't facing this life-altering commitment together when they barely knew each other.

Yes, they were compatible in bed—rather, in haylofts— but that didn't mean in her realistic, chaotic world they would mesh well. Added to that, she didn't know if *she* could handle having her passionate nature back in the public eye. Any serious relationship she took out in the open was subject to being exploited.

When they stepped into her trailer, Nash locked the door behind him. The cool air-conditioning greeted them. A small light from the tiny kitchenette had been left on, sending a soft glow throughout the narrow space.

Nash's heavy-lidded eyes met hers. She knew that look, had seen it nearly every night in person, then again in her dreams later. He could make a woman forget all about reality, all about responsibility.

This was the first time he'd been in her trailer and she realized just how broad and dominating his presence truly was. A shiver of arousal slid through her.

"We really should talk about this," she started, knowing she had lost control of this situation the moment she'd agreed to let him come back to her trailer. "I want you to know I didn't trap you."

"I know." He closed the gap between them, barely brushing his chest against hers. "I also know that I want you. I wanted you before you broke the news and I still do. A baby doesn't change the desire I have for you, Lily."

Oh, mercy. When he said things like that, when he looked at her like that…how could a girl think straight? Just one look from beneath those heavy lids framed by dark lashes had her body reacting before he could even touch her. This was why they had to sneak around. No way could she be in public with this man when he looked at her like he was ready to eat her up, and she knew she had that same passionate gaze when she looked at him.

He smelled all masculine and rugged, and pure hardworking man. A man who was gentle with animals and demanding as a lover was pretty much her greatest fantasy come to life. A fantasy she hadn't even known lived within her until she'd met Nash.

"Maybe we shouldn't be doing this," she stated as his fingertips slid up over her chest and started peeling away the elastic top of her dress. "I mean, we have a lot to talk about, right?"

Nash nodded, keeping his focus on his task. "We do,

but right now you're responding to my touch. I can't ignore that. Can you?"

His gaze met and trapped hers. "Unless you're ashamed to have the groom in your trailer."

Lily reached up, squeezing both of his hands. "I've never, ever hinted that I'm ashamed of you, Nash. I'm just not normally a fling girl and whatever we have going on is nobody else's business. That's all. I'm not hiding anything else."

A brief shadow crossed over his face and Lily wondered if she'd imagined it for a moment because just as fast as it came, it was gone.

"I can't deny you," she whispered. "How can this pull still be so strong?"

Nash dipped down, gliding his mouth over the curve of her neck, causing her head to fall back. The rasp of his beard against her bare skin always had tingles shooting all over her body. On occasion he'd trimmed his beard back, but thankfully he'd never fully shaved, because Lily figured she was ruined for smooth faces forever after being with Nash.

"Because passion is such a strong emotion," he murmured as his lips trailed up her neck. "And what we have is too fierce to sum up in one word."

In no time he'd yanked her dress down to pool at her feet. Lily kicked it aside as he quickly worked her free of her strapless bra and panties.

He reached behind his back and jerked his T-shirt up and over his head, tossing it to the side. Those chiseled muscles beneath a sprinkling of dark hair on his chest didn't come from working out in some air-conditioned gym. Nash's taut ripples came the old-fashioned way: from hours of manual labor.

"I love how you look at me," he muttered as he lifted her from the waist and crossed to the end of the trailer with the bed.

He lay her down and stood over her, whipping his belt through the loops of his jeans. Lily didn't know what on earth they were doing. Okay, she knew what they were doing, but wasn't this a mistake? Shouldn't they be discussing the baby? What their plans were for the future?

But when his weight settled over her, pushing her deeper into the thick comforter, Lily relished in the feel of his hard body molding perfectly with hers. Right here, this was the feeling she'd come to crave—the heaviness of him pressing into her in a protective, all-consuming manner.

Nash was right. *Passion* was such a simple word for the intensity of what they shared. But what label did it have? The impulse with which they'd jumped into an affair had overwhelmed them both. They'd never given anything beyond sex another thought.

The truth was, she had feelings for Nash, feelings she didn't think she'd have again for another man. Could she trust her feelings to stand up to public scrutiny? Could she rely on anything she felt that stemmed from a hidden affair?

Giving up her mental volley of trying to have this all make sense, Lily raked her fingers up his back and over his shoulders as he settled between her thighs. Nash had a way to make her forget everything around her, make her want to lock away the moments in time she shared with him. As he entered her, his mouth claimed hers and Lily had no choice but to surrender. Why did every moment with this man make her feel things she'd never felt before?

Nash's hands slid up her sides and over her breasts as her body arched into his. In no time her core responded, tightening as Nash continued to move with her.

After he followed her lead and their bodies stopped trembling, he lifted her in his arms, tucked her beneath the covers and climbed in beside her.

"Rest, Lily." He reached over and shut off the light. "Tomorrow we'll work this out."

Did he mean he'd still try to get her to move into his house? Although his dominance was a turn-on, she wouldn't let him just start taking charge simply because of the baby.

She was still in charge of her own life. Besides, being intimate with a man and living with him were two very different things.

As much as Nash was coming to mean to her, she still had to face reality. She was going to be done filming in about a week and she had a life in LA to get back to.

So where did that leave them?

Well, what a surprise. They'd ended up with their clothes off again and nothing was discussed or planned.

On the upside, she wasn't nauseous this morning…yet.

As she headed toward the makeup trailer, her new agent Ian Schaffer stepped out of one of the cottages on the Barrington estate. Ian had initially come out to the movie set in hopes of getting Lily to sign with his agency, and she did, but then he had gone and fallen in love with one of the beautiful Barrington sisters.

Sweet Cassie, the gentle trainer, and her precious girl, Emily, were both part of Ian's life now and family had never looked so adorable. Ian caught her eye and waved as he headed her way. At some point she'd have to discuss her own family situation with Ian and what this meant for upcoming films…especially since he was already getting several scripts for her to look over.

Too bad none of those movies called for a pukey pregnant heroine. She'd so nail that audition with her pasty complexion and random bouts of profuse sweating.

"You have a second?" he asked.

"Sure." Lily shifted so Ian's height blocked the morning sun. "We're heading into town today to shoot a scene near the flower shop, but I'm not due in wardrobe for a few more minutes. What's up?"

"I have a really good script that came through yesterday I'd like you to look at it." Ian rested his hands on his hips and smiled. "I know we've only worked together for a few weeks, but you had indicated that you'd like to try something different, maybe break away from the softer, family-style roles and into something more edgy. Are you still up for that?"

Lily tilted her head and shrugged. "Depends on the role and the producer. What do you have for me?"

"How would you feel about playing a showgirl who is a struggling single mother?"

Lily froze. "Um…yeah, that's quite the opposite of anything I've done before."

Oh the irony. Showgirl? By the time the movie started filming Lily figured her waistline would be nonexistent. As far as the single mom aspect? She honestly had no clue. Nash claimed he wouldn't leave her, but he'd only been aware of the baby for less than twenty-four hours. Once reality set in would he still feel the same?

"Lily?" Ian eased his head down until his gaze caught hers. "You all right? You don't have to look at the script if that's too far outside your comfort level, but I will say the producers are amazing and the script is actually very well plotted. Aiden O'Neil was just cast as the opposite lead."

Aiden was a great guy, an awesome actor and would be a joy to work with again. But how could she accept this role knowing she couldn't commit to the grueling hours of exercise and perfecting her body that, no doubt, Hollywood would require in order to portray a showgirl?

Lily's eyes drifted over Ian's shoulder and landed on Nash. Now that was a leading man…and he'd sneaked out of her trailer without her noticing. He'd promised to be gone by morning, and he was, but still she'd been a little disappointed not to be able to wake up next to him. Yes, she was quickly losing control over her feelings for Nash and she feared she'd have a hard time keeping them tucked against her heart.

Ian swiveled, glanced across the estate and turned back to Lily. "I'm not sure why you keep hiding what you two have going on."

Lily jerked her attention back to Ian. "Excuse me?"

Shrugging, Ian smiled. "I won't say anything, and honestly I doubt anyone else has picked up on the vibes you two are sending out."

Lily wasn't sure if she was relieved or afraid that someone else knew about her and Nash. Old images of a video she'd thought private played through her mind. That was another time, another man. Nash was trustworthy…wasn't he?

"What is it you think you know?" she asked, crossing her arms over her chest.

"I caught you two in a rather…comfortable embrace about a month ago. I was looking for Cassie and you and Nash were in the stables. I didn't say anything because I know you value your privacy and it was nobody's business what you two do in your downtime."

Lily had thought for sure no one would've spotted them at night and after hours. Thankfully it was only Ian who most definitely had her best interest at heart. As her agent, he didn't want any bad press surrounding her, either. The limelight would stay directed elsewhere, for now.

Blowing out a sigh, Lily nodded. "I don't know what is going on between Nash and me, to be honest. But just keep this between us, okay?"

Ian smiled. "You're my client, and I'd like to think, friend. We all have secrets, Lily. I won't say a word."

Speaking of secrets, she had a doozy. But for now, she would keep the pregnancy to herself. This was definitely something she and Nash needed to work through before sharing the announcement with any outsiders. They were still riding the sexual high, the excitement of being so physically attracted to each other, she had no clue how to discuss something so permanent with him. They were facing a relationship she didn't think either of them was ready for.

"You sure you're okay?" Ian asked.

Pulling out her most convincing smile, Lily nodded and turned to head toward the wardrobe trailer. "Fine. Just ready to relax after this shoot is over."

"Well, when you get a chance, come find me. I'll let you

look over those scripts." He fell into step with her. "I believe the single mom part would be perfect for you, but that's going to depend on how comfortable you are with playing a show-girl. I also have a part that is set in a mythical world, and that also involves bearing a great deal of skin because from what I can see, the women all wear bikini tops and short skirts."

Lily refrained from groaning because here she was, just discovering her pregnancy and already having to choose between her career and her personal life.

How would she juggle this all when the baby came? Eventually the world would know she was pregnant, then she couldn't keep Nash a secret any longer—couldn't keep her feelings for him a secret. Sooner rather than later, their relationship—whatever it became—would be out front and center.

How would he cope? How would they get through this? As a couple? As two people just sharing a child? With the depth of her feelings only growing stronger, Lily worried she was in for a long road of heartache.

Three

It was after midnight and Lily hadn't come to him. He'd spent the night in her trailer, in her arms. So why wasn't she here?

Turning off the lights in the stables, Nash kept to the shadows of the property and headed toward the back of the estate where Lily's trailer sat. He told himself he just wanted to check on her to make sure she was feeling okay. Nash refused to believe he was developing deeper feelings for her. He couldn't afford to be sidetracked right now, not until his plan was fully executed.

He climbed the two steps and glanced over his shoulder to double-check he was alone before giving her door a couple taps with his knuckles. When she didn't answer, he tried the handle, surprised it turned easily beneath his palm. Even with security, keeping the door unlocked wasn't smart. You never knew what length the crazies would go to in order to snap a picture of a celebrity. Money held more power than people gave it credit for.

"You need to keep this locked," he told her as he entered. "Anybody could walk right in."

Lily sat hunched over the small dinette table, papers

spread all around her. When she glanced up at him, tear tracks marred her creamy cheeks.

Fear gripped him as he crossed the small space. "Lily, what happened? Is it the baby?"

Raking her hands through her long, dark hair, she shook her head. "No, no. The baby is fine."

A slight sense of relief swept through him, but still, something was wrong. He'd never seen such fierce emotions from the woman who always appeared so flawless, so in control…except when she surrendered herself to him and she unleashed all of that pent-up passion.

"Then what is it?" he asked, sliding in beside her on the narrow booth.

Her hand waved across the table. "All of this. I'm looking at the future of my career, yet I have no clue what way to go. I'm at a crossroads, Nash, and I'm scared. There's no good answer."

Nash wrapped his arm around her and pulled her against his side. He'd grown used to the perfect feel of her petite body nestled next against his. What he wasn't used to was consoling a woman, delving into feelings beyond the superficial. This was definitely out of his comfort zone and he absolutely hated it. Hated how he'd allowed himself to get in this position of being vulnerable with the threat of being exposed before he was ready.

More than anything else, he hated lying to Lily. She didn't deserve to be pulled into his web of deceit and lies, but now that she was pregnant, there was no other option. He'd already put his plan in motion and he wasn't leaving until Damon Barrington gave up the horses and Nash disclosed his real identity to the man. Nash couldn't wait to see Damon's face when the truth was revealed.

But now he had Lily and a baby to worry about. He sure as hell didn't want innocents caught in the mix. Things had been so simple before, when Lily planned to wrap up filming and go on her way. Everything in her life from this moment on would revolve around their child and he had to figure out a way to make this right…he just had no clue how.

Angst rolled through him at the thought of his own mother feeling even an inkling of what Lily was going through. And his mother had been all on her own. No way would he ever let Lily feel as if she didn't have him to lean on. He wasn't looking for that traditional family, but he wouldn't abandon what was his.

For so long it had been just Nash and his mother. She'd always put his needs first, rarely dating, never bringing a man to the house until Nash was in his late teens when she got engaged and eventually married. She'd always made sure her two jobs covered their bills and a few extras.

In short, she worked her ass off, purposely setting her own needs aside until Nash was old enough to understand and care for himself.

He didn't want to see Lily struggling as a single mother, juggling a career and a child.

Added to that, she was pregnant with *his* child. It would take death to tear him away from what belonged to him. Did he love her? No. Love wasn't in the cards for him, wasn't something he believed in. That didn't mean he didn't already love this child they'd created. Now Nash had to make sure once she discovered the truth, she wouldn't shut him out.

He knew how she loathed liars, how she'd been betrayed by a man in her past. Surely she would see this situation was completely different.

"What are all these papers that have you so upset?" he asked her.

Lily rested a hand on his thigh, tapping a stack with her finger. "Scripts Ian gave me to look over for the next film. He's so excited because this will be our first film together, but everything here would be impossible for me to do until after the baby is born and that's if I get my body back. Hollywood is ruthless when it comes to added pounds."

He kept his opinion about Hollywood and their warped

sense of "beautiful" to himself. Not all women needed to be rails to be stunning and added pounds didn't take away from a woman's talents. Lily was a petite woman, but she had curves in all the right places.

"Why don't you tell Ian that none of these will work for you?"

Lily lazily drew an invisible pattern over his jeans with her fingertips. "I need to tell him about the baby. This has to be my sole focus. My career will have to come second for a while. I only hope I'm not committing career suicide."

Nash smiled and stroked away a strand of hair from her eyes. "I highly doubt this will kill your career. Ian will understand, I'm sure."

Lily scrubbed her hands over her face. "This is my life. I don't know anything else. What do I know about being a mom?"

About as much as he knew about being a dad.

She slid out the other side of the booth and grabbed a bottle of water from the fridge. Nash watched as she twisted off the cap and took a long drink. An overwhelming sense of possession swept through him. This sexy, vibrant woman would soon start showing visible signs of their secret affair.

"You can't keep pushing yourself right now, Lily. It's best you relax."

Her eyes darted to his. "I don't need you coming in here and telling me how I should be reacting. My life is mine alone, Nash. Yes, you're the baby's father, but I need to figure out what to do here. Even if I take some time off, I'm still in the spotlight. I don't want…"

She bit her lip and glanced away. In the soft light casting a glow in the narrow space, Nash saw another fresh set of tears swimming in her eyes. Damn it.

"You don't want the media to know," he murmured.

After a slight hesitation, she nodded, but still didn't meet his gaze. He climbed out of the seat and came up behind her, cupping her shoulders and easing her back against his chest.

"They're going to find out, Lily. What you need to do is make sure you always stay in control." Sliding his arms down, he covered her flat stomach with his hands, still in awe that a life grew inside there. "Don't let them start the gossip. I'm sure you have TV interviews scheduled. Make a big bombshell announcement then. You'll take the wind right out of the press's sails."

Lily turned in his arms. Her eyes met his as she blinked back tears. "That may be the best plan of action. But, I need to tell my mother first."

Her mother. They'd never discussed their parents. That topic usually meant a relationship was building. He and Lily hadn't planned on building on anything. They were enjoying their time together, not thinking of tomorrow.

Tomorrow, however, had caught up with them and smacked them in the face with a good dose of reality.

The fact they were bound forever now sent a bit of uncontrollable fear sliding through him. Whether either of them liked it or not, they were about to delve into personal territory.

Lily could talk about her mother all she wanted. That was most definitely an area in his life he wasn't ready to reveal.

"Does your mother live in LA, too?"

"No, she lives in Arizona in a small, private community that's run by an assisted living facility. She has her own home on the grounds and she's very independent, but if her health gets bad or as she gets older and needs care, she's already set."

Lily stepped back and crossed her arms. "I don't tell people where she is because I want her to have a normal life and not be hassled by the media."

Nash didn't want another reason to be drawn to Lily, but damn it she was protective of her mother. How could he not relate to that? Nash would do anything for his mother…which was why he was still harboring his secret instead of bursting through Damon's front doors and laying it all out on the line.

Part of Nash wished he'd never kept this secret about his life, wished he'd just confronted his past immediately and moved on. But he'd wanted to protect his mother and wanted to move cautiously without making rash decisions. Lily was a different story. He'd seen her, he'd wanted her. Now, here they were, pregnant and discussing parents.

Irony shot at him from so many angles he could hardly keep up. He had been a secret baby, and Lily was expecting a baby that had to remain a secret for now. The best course of action for him would be to complete his original plans and confront Damon.

"Are you going to see your mom as soon as you're done filming here?" he asked.

He needed her gone. He needed her away so he could have a face-to-face with Damon and not have Lily right there witnessing his confession of every single lie he'd told since meeting her. There was no way he could avoid the outcome, but he could at least soften the blow if she weren't present for the bomb he would drop.

He wanted so much, from Damon, from himself...from Lily. In the end, he would have it all. He hadn't gotten this far in his life by sitting idly by and watching opportunities pass. He reached with both hands and took what he wanted.

"I just need to think." She rubbed her head and sighed. "I need to find a doctor. I have no idea where to go. Obviously I should look in LA, but I won't be back there for a while."

"I'll find you one." When she quirked a brow, he added, "I know people in the area. You need a checkup and then you can see a doctor when you get home."

Assuming she went back home after filming wrapped up. Hell, he had no idea what her plans were. Honestly, all they'd managed to work out was how well they fit together intimately. Any discussion beyond that would be a vast change of pace.

"Just get me a name," she told him. "It's going to be nearly impossible to get in and out of a doctor's office here without word getting out about my condition."

Nash's mind was working overtime. He couldn't say too much or she'd know something was off about him and who she believed he was. She had to keep thinking he was just a groom until he could tell her otherwise. The last thing he needed at this point was her, or anyone for that matter, getting suspicious. Still, money talked and he'd use any means necessary to get her the proper care she needed while she was here.

"I bet we could get a doctor to come here, secretly," he offered. "People can be silenced for a price."

Lily's eyes widened. "You're not paying someone to keep quiet. I know how this works, Nash. We just need to find someone who can be discreet."

From her tone and the worry filling her eyes, Nash knew she didn't like the idea of him spending his money on her health care. Little did she know how heavily padded his accounts were. Even if they weren't, even if he did only make groom's wages, he'd spend every last cent if that meant proper care for his baby.

"I'll take care of it," he assured her. "You won't have to worry about a thing."

Lily leaned her shoulder against the narrow kitchenette cabinet and stared at him. "There are so many layers to you," she muttered. "You're all casual and laid-back, yet sometimes you're all business and take-charge. Makes me wonder who the real Nash is."

She'd barely scratched the surface. All too soon those layers would be peeled back one at a time, revealing things that would change lives forever.

Forcing himself to relax, he hooked his thumbs through his belt loops, intending to keep playing the part of groom. "Which Nash do you think I am?"

With a shrug, Lily continued to stare. "I'm not sure. You

just seem more, I don't know, powerful and composed than I thought you'd be about the baby."

In one stride he'd closed the space between them, snaked his arms around her waist and leaned over her so her back arched. "You saying I wasn't powerful when we were in the loft?"

Lily's hands slid up his chest. "Oh, you were powerful, but you didn't have that serious tone you just used."

Nash eyed her mouth, then traveled back up to her eyes. "Trust me, when it comes to someone I care about, I'm very serious."

Lily's tremble vibrated his entire body. He couldn't let her know anything about his real life, but at the same time he had to use his influences to keep her near, keep her and the baby safe. Everything in his life was at stake—things he hadn't even considered a possibility were now major markers on his journey. He'd started down this path with one vision, now suddenly there were forks in the road. Still, he had to stay on track because no matter which way he went, hearts would be ripped apart. Two life-altering secrets would shatter the trust he'd built with everyone around him over the past couple of months.

Even with the odds drastically stacked against him, with the devil in the corner mocking him, Nash had no intention of failing. He'd have it all: the horses, a family, his baby.

Four

"What do you mean he's still not accepting our offer?"

Nash glanced behind him, making sure he was still alone. He'd stepped out of the stables and around the side where he was sure to have privacy when his assistant had called.

Damon Barrington may technically be his boss here, but Nash had a surprise in store for him.

"I know what they're planning," Nash said in a low tone. "I know exactly what he's willing to let go of and what he wants to hold on to. What the hell will it take to get him to sell to me?"

"I think that's the issue," his assistant replied. "You know how he feels about you. He may sell to someone else."

Nash raked a hand through his hair. Yeah, he knew how Damon felt about him. They'd been ongoing rivals in the horse industry and for the past two years or so, but they'd pretty much used their assistants to handle all business dealings between them. That gap in time had only aided in Nash's covert plans. All he'd done was grow a beard, grow his hair longer and put on old, well-worn clothes. Sometimes the easiest way to hide things, or people, was right in plain sight.

Nash had wanted to purchase several of Damon's prize-winning horses, knowing the mogul was set to retire after this season, but Damon kept refusing. Nash needed those horses, needed the bloodlines on his own estate because he'd not been faring well in the races and losing was not an option.

The most recent offer had been exorbitant and Damon still wasn't budging. Stubborn man.

Like father, like son.

"Let me think," Nash said, heading back toward the front of the stables. "I'll call you back."

He slid the phone into his pocket and rounded the corner. Stepping from the shade to the vibrant sun had him pulling his cowboy hat down lower. He needed to figure out what it would take to get Damon to sell those horses to him because Nash had never taken no for an answer and he sure as hell wouldn't start now.

Pulling the pitchfork off the hook on the wall, Nash set out to clean out the stalls at the end of the aisle. Tessa and Cassie had taken two of the coveted horses out for a bit which gave him time to think and work without distractions.

What if someone else called Damon's assistant and made an offer? Would the tenacious man consider the generous offer then if he knew the horses weren't going to his rival?

Nash shoved the pitchfork into the hay, scooped out the piles and tossed them into the wheelbarrow. He missed his own estate, missed doing the grunt work with his own horses, in his own lavish stables. But he'd left his groom in charge and knew he could trust the man.

Only Nash's assistant knew where he was and that he was trying to spy on the Barringtons in an attempt to buy them out. But even his right-hand man wasn't aware of the other secret that had Nash uncovered here. Nobody knew and until he was ready to disclose his full plan, he had to keep it that way.

If Damon hated him before, how would the elderly man feel once he discovered the real truth?

By the time the first stall was clean, sweat trickled down his back. Nash pulled his hat off, tugged his T-shirt over his head and slapped his hat back on. He didn't often take his shirt off during workdays, but the day was almost done and the heat was stifling. He'd even gotten used to the itchiness of his beard after endless hours of working in this heat.

After both stalls were ready to go, Nash put all the materials away. Damon kept a clean, neat stable—something they had in common.

Nash didn't want to admit they had anything in common, but over the past several months since he had been on the Barrington estate, he'd seen Damon many times, seen how he treated his family, the crew filming there. But Nash hadn't allowed himself to get swept into that personal realm. He was here for a job, both as a groom and as a businessman.

Nash's last order of business was sweeping the walkway, ridding it of the stray straw and dust. The chore didn't take long, but had him sweating even more. He pulled the T-shirt from his back pocket and swiped it across his neck and chest.

"Have you ever thought of doing calendars?"

Nash jerked around to see the object of his every desire standing in the stable entryway, the sunlight illuminating her rich hair, her curvy build.

"What are you doing here?"

"Is Cassie around?"

"She's out riding." He took a step closer, since no one was around and he couldn't resist. So, he'd actually found one thing he had absolutely no control over. "You all right?"

With a soft smile, she nodded. "Yeah. I have a short break between scenes and I needed to ask her something."

Fisting his shirt, Nash crossed his arms over his chest. "Care to elaborate?"

"I'm asking her what doctor she used while she was pregnant, if you must know," she whispered.

"I already found out and you have an appointment." He'd had to do some sneaky digging, or rather his assistant did, but he'd been able to find the doctor in town who Cassie had seen for her pregnancy. "I was going to tell you this evening because I wasn't sure of your schedule today."

Her eyes raked over his bare chest and he didn't mind one bit being the recipient of her visual lick. "Keep looking at me like that and people are going to know more about us than we want them to."

Her eyes snapped up to his. "I can't even think when you're working like that," she muttered, gaze darting back down to his bare chest. "But thank you for arranging the doctor. When is he coming?"

"*She* will be here on Thursday."

Lily nodded. "That will be great. We're supposed to finish filming Thursday, but they may have something else for me to do last minute. I'll make sure I'm free, though."

"We're meeting at my house so there's no question as to why she's here."

"Taking control again?" A corner of Lily's lips kicked up into a grin. "This once I don't mind and if we were alone, I'd show you how grateful I am for you taking care of this."

Damn, his body responded immediately and he couldn't wait to get back to her trailer. "We'll be alone later and I'll let you."

At first all the sneaking around had been exciting, thrilling. Of course, that part was still arousing, but they basically knew nothing about each other. All he'd wanted was to confront his past, secure his future and now he was dealing with a whole new future.

Lily was an amazing woman, there was no denying that fact. But that didn't make him ready to settle down and play house, either. Could he see himself with someone like her? Considering they only knew each other in the bedroom, sure. Reality might be a different story.

Why the hell was he thinking like this? They were having a baby, that didn't mean they had to register for monogrammed towels.

"Hey, Lily."

Nash turned to see the beautiful Barrington sisters as they led their horses into the stalls.

"Hi, Cassie, Tessa." Lily walked around him, sending her signature scent of lilac straight through him. "I had a break from filming and thought I'd come see you guys since I rarely get in here."

Good save.

Nash went on with his duties, trying to ignore the feminine laughter of the three women in his life…only two of them had no clue just how close to him they were.

He'd created a complete and utter mess and he had to gain control and figure out how the hell to keep his plans and deception from blowing up in his face.

As much as he didn't want to admit it, he'd come to care for this family. Even though he hadn't let them in beyond work, he knew these sisters, saw the love their father had for them, witnessed bonding moments when they thought no one was around.

They were a family. A tight-knit, perfectly woven-together family. And when Nash ended up besting Damon, Nash had no clue where that would leave him in the family tree.

Ridding her body of her meager breakfast of dry toast was not a promising start to her day. It was the final day of shooting and Lily just wanted to crawl back into bed and tell the crew to do the scene without her. With her stomach revolting, she didn't care that she was the female lead, she just wanted to lie in her bed and die, because she was positive that's what was happening.

She was already fifteen minutes late for hair and makeup. She was never late. Some actors and actresses had a reputation for being divas while filming, often times making the rest of the crew wait on them, but Lily had prided herself on being professional. Her time wasn't worth any more than any other person's on set.

She slapped her sunglasses on, hoping to hide the dark

circles until she got to the makeup chair. She'd had enough energy to throw on her strapless maxi dress and flip-flops before heading out. But her mind wasn't on filming. Besides the baby, Lily was seriously starting to worry about her and Nash.

Her and Nash? Why did they instantly click like a couple inside her mind?

Because that's the way her mind—and her heart—had started leaning. The man exuded strength, not just in his physical job, but with everything he did. Since he found out about the baby he'd been ready to control every aspect of this pregnancy, to anticipate her every need. And, as much as it pained her to admit it, his dominating presence only deepened her attraction to him.

There was so much to the man and she wanted to discover it all. She completely trusted him with her body, now she wanted to see if she could trust him with more.

What did he want? Did he want more with her? If he did, would he be able to handle the very public life she led? One worry after another cycled through her head.

The overcast clouds were about as cheery and pleasant as she felt at the moment. She really hoped the first trimester passed quickly and she was a textbook case pregnancy because, while she was excited about the little life growing inside her, she was so over feeling carsick, as if she was riding a roller coaster and spinning in circles all at once.

Adding all of that to the uncertainty about Nash and what move they would take next was about to break her.

"I was just coming to check on you." Ian fell into step beside her. "Everything okay?"

Tears pricked her eyes. Was everything okay? Not really. She was pregnant by a man she knew little about and she was falling in love with him. That chaotic mess had somehow become her life and she had no clue how to sort out all these emotions to make sense of things.

Ian stared at her, waiting on her to answer. Shoving her

hair away from her shoulders, Lily blinked back tears, thankful for the sunglasses.

"I wasn't feeling very well this morning."

He gripped her elbow and pulled her gently to a stop. "You're looking a little pale. Are you okay?"

Lily sniffed and shook her head. "No, I'm not, but I will be."

Ian's brows drew together as he glanced around, then focused back on her. "You're crying. That's not okay. Did something happen with your mom?"

"No, my mom is fine."

Lily reached beneath her sunglasses and swiped the tips of her fingers at the tears just starting to escape. Why couldn't she control her emotions? She just wanted to wrap up this day of filming and go back to her trailer where she could think of how to gently let Nash know she was developing stronger feelings for him.

"If you're sick, maybe I should see about putting your scene off. A few more hours shouldn't make a difference."

A few hours? She needed a few weeks, or months, depending on how long this state of feeling like death lingered. Of course by that time she'd resemble a whale which would totally knock her out of playing Rose Barrington.

"A few hours won't make a difference, but thanks."

She sniffed again, desperately needing a tissue. Wow, if the paparazzi could only see her now. Sniffling, crying and looking like pure hell. They'd make up something akin to Starlet Hooked on Drugs or The Girl Next Door Reverts Back to Her Wild Days as their top story.

"Does this have to do with Nash?" he whispered. "You seem really upset for just not feeling well. Did he do something?"

Hysterical laughter burst through her as more tears flowed. Yeah, she was officially a disaster and she was totally falling apart in front of her new agent. An agent who had flown all the way out here to convince her to sign with his agency…the poor man was probably reconsidering his decision even though in the short time they'd been official, they had come to think of each other as good friends.

So instead of letting him continue to think she'd gone completely insane, she blurted out, "I'm pregnant."

Ian's eyes widened for only a second before he wrapped his arm around her shoulder and pulled her into a friendly hug.

"I assume this is Nash's?"

Lily nodded against his shoulder and held on to his arms. "Nobody knows. Please keep the news to yourself until I tell you otherwise."

"Of course." He gave her shoulder a slight squeeze, then stepped back. "Is this why you haven't gotten back to me on either of those scripts?"

His smile warmed her and she nodded. "I'm so torn. I have no clue what work you can find for me and I just don't know how I'll manage with being pregnant or even what will happen when the baby comes."

Ian kept his grip on her shoulders and tipped his head down to look her straight in the eye. "Listen, this news is a shock to you now, but you are a strong woman. Actresses have babies all the time. You will do just fine and I've no doubt I'll find work for you. Never worry about that. That's my job. Okay?"

The strong wind had her hair dancing around her shoulders. Lily shoved the wayward strands behind her ears. "I need to get to hair and makeup. I'm really late now. Thanks for understanding and for keeping my secret."

Ian dropped his hands. "You go on. I'm going to see Nash because he's been shooting death glares at me from the stables since we stopped to talk."

Wrapping her arms around her waist, Lily smiled. "He's a bit protective."

"Looks like a man in love to me."

Love? No. Lust? Yes. They weren't near the stage for love to enter the equation—well, she was teetering on the brink. Their sexual chemistry was completely off the charts, though.

"Tell him I'll see him later and that I'm fine," she told Ian. "He worries like my mother."

With a soft chuckle, Ian nodded. "Will do."

Ian walked toward the stables and Lily paused briefly to stare at Nash. Even from across the wide concrete drive and the side yard, she could see the stone-solid look on his face. That wasn't jealousy. What did he have to be jealous of, anyway? Yes, they were having a baby together, but they'd still made no commitment to each other.

Why shouldn't they try for more? Why couldn't she just tell him what she wanted? She wasn't asking for a ring on her finger. This innocent baby wouldn't be caught in the middle. Lily wanted her child to have security and the love of both parents whether they were together or not. She had to figure out how Nash felt about her beyond the sexual aspect.

But she had a feeling she knew how his mind worked. A man like Nash wouldn't let go of anything that belonged to him and since this baby was his, she knew he wouldn't let go of her, either.

This could be an opportunity to see if she was ready for something long-term with the man who had literally turned her world upside down.

Five

Nash had no idea how nervous he had been about this appointment until he closed the door behind the doctor once the checkup was done. Now he and Lily were alone in his rental house which was only a few miles from the Barrington estate.

The baby was healthy with a good, strong heartbeat. Lily's blood pressure was a bit on the high side and the doctor warned about too much stress and urged her to rest for the next few weeks until the next appointment. Nash vowed silently to make sure Lily was relaxed, pampered and wanted for nothing as long as she was here. And she would stay here for the next few weeks...if not longer. They hadn't really discussed her living arrangements, but Nash wasn't backing down on this matter. His child would stay under his roof for now.

The movie had officially wrapped up yesterday and Lily was free. Which meant he had some decisions to make. This wasn't just about Nash and Lily anymore. An innocent baby would be coming into this world soon and would depend on his or her parents to provide a stable, loving home.

When he stepped back into the living room, Lily was reclining on the leather chaise in the corner, pointing the remote toward the flat screen hanging above the stone mantel. He may be using this home as a prop for his plan, but that didn't mean he couldn't decorate it according to his style and his needs, just on a smaller scale. His designer had done quick work before Nash moved in and everything was perfect for a single groom who splurged only on a few necessities. A large television was a necessity.

When Lily had mentioned how nice his home was, he'd indicated the place came already furnished. A small lie piled atop all the others he'd doled out since he'd put his plan into motion. At this point, what was a white lie about decor in the grand scheme of things?

Lily's vibrant eyes shot to his, a smile spread across her face as he approached. "I know I should still be scared, or nervous, or whatever, but I'm just so happy the baby is healthy."

Resting his hip next to her bare legs on the chaise, Nash settled his hand on her calf and rubbed from her ankle to her knee. "There's no rule book that states you have to feel a certain way."

Lily rested her head against the arm, her hair falling over her shoulder, framing her natural beauty. This was how he preferred her. Not made up for a shoot with perfectly sprayed hair, but fresh-faced, hair down and wearing a casual dress. He loved how she didn't worry about her looks, didn't fuss with herself just because she came from the land where appearances were more valuable than talent.

Small-town life suited her and Nash wasn't immune to the fact he was starting to like how well she blended into his world…or the world he'd created for his charade.

How would she look in his real home? In his grand master suite that had a balcony overlooking the fields? The need to make love to her beneath the dark sky slammed into him. He wanted her on his estate, not in the rental home that was merely a prop for a life that wasn't even his.

"I'm pretty calm right now." She rested her hand on his

thigh, her dainty pink polish striking against his dark denim. "The film is done, the baby is fine."

Lily's hand came up, her fingertip traveled over the area between his brows. "Why the worry lines?"

Where to start? Did he confess now that he'd lied about his identity all along? Did he tell her he had more money than she ever thought possible and that this house, even his name, was one giant cover to keep him trudging forward with his master plan?

Did he truly want to see all that hurt in her eyes when he came clean about his life, that nearly every single thing he'd ever told her had been false?

Damn it, he hated he'd become *that* man. Hated that he would inevitably crush her. He didn't want her to look at him in disgust, but the moment would come and there wasn't a damn thing he could do about it. All he could do was stall, earn her trust outside of the bedroom.

Whether he wanted to face the fact or not, his feelings for her were growing deeper and damn if that didn't complicate things even further.

He'd thought getting her out of his system, then out of his life after the film was over, would be a piece of cake. His secrets could've remained just that from her and he could've revealed them once she was gone.

Yet here he was, tangled in his own web of lies, becoming more and more restricted with each passing day, each new lie, and finding himself sinking deeper into a woman he knew only intimately.

"Just worried about you." And that was the absolute truth. "With your blood pressure on the high side, I just want to make sure you take it easy."

Her hand slid over his stubbled cheek. "I'm taking it easy right now."

Easing forward, craving more of her touch, Nash slid his hand up over her knee, beneath the soft cotton dress and over her thigh. "I intend for you to take it easy until your next appointment."

Lily stilled, her hand falling into her lap. "Nash, I can't stay that long. I have a life in LA, a job, my mother is in Arizona...I can't just stay here and forget all of my obligations."

"You can take a break," he insisted. "You heard the doctor. A month off will be good for you and you don't have another film to get to, right?"

Lily shrugged, her eyes darting to her lap where she toyed with the bunched material of her dress. "I can't stay here with you, Nash. This baby is real. I can't just play house."

"You can." His eyes held hers as he leaned closer, nipped her lips and eased back. "You can stay for today." He nipped again. "And tomorrow."

He wasn't ready to play house yet, either, but he also wasn't letting her go.

"Reality is so hard to face when you're touching me," she murmured against his lips. "I don't even know what to do next."

Nash eased back and winked. "I've got a good idea."

"Does it involve the kitchen?" she asked with a crooked grin.

Giving her thigh a squeeze, Nash leaned back. "I thought you were nauseous?"

"Right now I'm starving."

Nash came to his feet and glanced down to her. The way she all but stretched out over the chaise, her dress hitched up to near indecent level, her hair spread all around her, she was sexy personified and had no clue the power she held.

And she was pregnant with his child. He never imagined just how much of a turn-on that would be.

Mine. That's all he could think right at this moment and the revelation nearly had his knees buckling

"What are you in the mood for?" he asked, trying to focus.

"Grilled cheese."

"Grilled cheese? Like bread, butter and a lot of fatty cheese?"

"You saying I can't have that?" she asked, quirking a brow as if daring him to argue.

"Not at all." With a laugh, he held his hands up in defense. "I'm just shocked that's what you're asking for."

"Grilled cheese is just one of my weaknesses," she told him. "All that gooey cheese and crispy bread."

Something so simple, yet a fact he hadn't known about her. Which just proved he really didn't know much about the mother of his child except how to excite her, how to get her to make those sweet little moans, how to make her lids flutter down just before she climaxed.

"One grilled cheese coming right up," he declared, quickly heading toward the kitchen before he took what he wanted, which was Lily all laid out beneath him.

He was serious about wanting her there, wanting her to stay with him until they figured out a game plan. So that meant he needed to take the time to learn more about her and not just how fast he could peel down those strapless sundresses she seemed so fond of.

As much as he wanted to learn about her, he was terrified she'd be wanting to learn more about him.

Which begged the ultimate question. Did he come clean or continue this farce for as long as possible?

Ever the gentleman, Nash had put her bags from her on-site trailer in his guest bedroom. He was giving her the option of staying in a room by herself or sleeping with him.

This baby had them taking every step carefully, moving from a hot, steamy affair into something more...calm.

Lily slid her hand over her still-flat stomach and took in the cozy bedroom with its pale gray walls, dark furniture and navy bedding. The fact that she was pregnant with his child and trying to figure out where to sleep was really absurd.

Lily turned, smacking into the hard, firm wall of Nash's

chest. His bare, gloriously naked, tanned, taut muscular chest. Would she ever tire of looking at this man? Would her body's fierce response always be so overwhelming? When she was with Nash she couldn't think, let alone figure out a future or make decisions. He aroused her, made her ache and crave his touch, and he'd managed to start working his way into her heart. Strong, firm hands gripped her bare arms in an attempt to steady her as her eyes held on to the tantalizing view before her.

"I'm going to assume by the way you're looking at me that you're not sleeping in the guest room."

Lily's eyes traveled up to see the smirk, the dark lifted brows. "Did you parade in here half-naked on purpose to sway my decision?"

With his focus on her lips, the tips of his fingertips slid over her sensitive breasts and down her torso to grip her hips and pull her flush against his strong body.

"It wouldn't take much persuasion to get you in my bed," he murmured against her lips. "The decision up to you."

She never grew tired of his hard body against hers. Lily flattened her palms against his chest. "I'd love to sleep in your bed, but I need you to know that I have no clue what's happening between us. I mean, I know I have feelings for you that go beyond sex. And that was before the baby. I don't know what to do now and I have no clue how you're feeling."

Great, now she was babbling and had turned into that woman who needed emotional reassurance. She'd also exposed herself a bit more than she'd intended.

Shaking her head, she slid her arms up around his neck and laced her fingers together. "Never mind. I'm not looking for you to say anything or make some grand declaration. I guess I'm just still scarred from trusting the wrong man a long time ago."

Of course she'd redeemed herself, but Lily had no doubt if she slipped up the media would be all too quick to resurrect that footage her then "boyfriend" had taken of her in the bedroom.

"You can trust me," Nash told her, sliding his hands up and down her back. "I know you're worried about the future, but you can trust that I will always take care of you and our baby. Never doubt that."

The strong conviction in his tone had her believing every word he said. "You must've had some really amazing parents for you to be so determined and loyal."

A sliver of pain flashed through those icy blue eyes. "My mother was the strongest woman I've ever known. She's the driving force behind everything good in my life."

"And your father?"

Nash swallowed as he paused. Silence hovered between them and Lily realized she probably should just learn to keep her mouth shut. But she wanted to know more about Nash. He was the father of her child, for pity's sake. They were bound together for life and eventually, little by little, they had to start opening up. "I never knew my father."

Lily's heart broke for him as she smoothed his messy hair away from his face. "I'm sorry. My father passed when I was younger, so I know a little about that void."

Click. Another bond locked into place and her heart slid another notch toward falling for this man.

"So it was just you and your mother, too?"

That scenario would've been better, actually. After all she and her mother had lived through, being alone would've been for the best.

"No." Lily slid from his arms and went to her bag to pull out a nightgown. She hated discussing her stepfather. "My mother was a proud woman, but we were pretty poor and she ended up marrying for financial stability."

A shrink would love diving into her head. The stepfather had virtually ruined her for any man with money and power. Settling down with someone as controlling as that wasn't an option. Lily would rather be alone than to be told how to live her life.

Lily kept her back to Nash as she pulled her strapless maxi dress down to puddle at her feet before she tugged her silky chemise on. For now her sexy clothes still fit.

"She probably wouldn't have married Dan had it not been for me," she told him, turning back around. "Mom was worried how she would keep our house, keep up her two jobs and keep food and clothes coming."

Picking up her discarded dress, she laid it on the bed and crossed back to Nash. "He was a jerk to her. Treated her like a maid instead of a wife. Treated me like I didn't even exist, which was fine because I didn't want a relationship with him anyway. But I loathe him for how he treated my mother."

Nash pulled her into his arms, surrounding her with the warmth and security she'd hardly known. This sense of stability was something she could easily get used to, but could she trust her emotions right now? Passion was one thing, but to fully rely on someone else, to trust with her whole heart… she wanted that more than anything.

"He's probably sorry he treated you like that now that you're famous."

Lily laughed and eased back to look him in the eyes. "I wouldn't know. He left my mother several years ago, just as I was getting my start. He took all the money, even what she'd worked for. He was always a greedy money whore. Money never meant anything to me, still doesn't. It doesn't define me, but I saw the evil it produced."

Nash's arms tightened on her again. "Money isn't evil, Lily. It's what a person chooses to do with it that can be evil."

"Yeah, well I choose to keep my mother comfortable in a nice home that's in a gated community where she can have her privacy and not worry. Other than that, I don't need it."

"So if I were a rich man you wouldn't have looked my way twice?" he joked.

Lily laughed. "Oh, you still would've caught my attention. I've just always promised myself I wouldn't get involved with anyone like my stepfather."

Nash squeezed her tighter. "Not all men are like your stepfather."

"Don't defend him."

Nash's chuckle vibrated through her. "I'm not, baby. I'm defending all of mankind."

Lily snuggled deeper into his embrace, wondering what path they were starting down. The last time her passion had bested her, she'd ended up across the internet, on the news and every magazine willing to make money off her bad decisions. Karma had intervened and her ex hadn't made it very far in the industry. She couldn't help but take a little satisfaction.

Now her passion had cornered her again. This time the consequences were far greater than a soiled reputation. She was going to be in charge of another life. How long would Nash want to be in the baby's life? Would he honestly be a hands-on father? He hadn't grown up with a dad so perhaps he truly did want to give this child a better life.

Lily hated all the unknowns that surrounded them, but her doctor said she needed to relax and she would do anything to ensure a healthy baby. Maybe she hadn't planned on a child, but the reality was, she was going to have one. There was a little being inside of her right now with a heartbeat of its own, growing each and every day. Angry as she may be at herself for allowing this to happen, she couldn't deny that she loved this baby already. If that meant relaxing with Nash for the next several weeks or even months, she wouldn't argue.

She'd wondered how they would work if they tried for something more serious, more than just ripping each other's clothes off at every opportunity. How would they mesh together in reality?

Looked like she was about to get her chance to find out.

Six

He was screwed. Royally, utterly screwed. He'd wanted to open up to her, wanted to start paving the way for an honest relationship. Or at least some type of relationship, considering she was carrying his child and he was developing stronger feelings for her.

Nash still couldn't put a title on whatever they had going because all their "relationship" consisted of so far was hot, fast sex in a stable loft and a surprise baby. He didn't know what the hell the next logical step would be because nothing about the entire past two months had been logical.

But Lily deserved the truth and Nash was too much of a coward to give it to her. He'd had an opening last night when they'd been halfway clothed and just talking. Such an emotionally intimate moment hadn't happened between them before, but that moment slipped by about as quickly as he'd taken off her silky gown. Yet again, he'd let passion override anything else. His need to have her consumed him and he didn't even try to push it aside and reveal his secrets.

Desire was easier to deal with than the harsh realities waiting them both.

Even when she'd spent the night in his bed, he had time to open up. Yet here he was making breakfast on a Saturday

morning like some domestic family man when so many secrets hovered between them.

Soon, he'd reveal the truth—or at least all he was able to.

Damn it. He wanted more from her than sex. He hadn't
expected this…whatever "this" was. The fact so many lies
lay between them only cheapened anything they would start
to build together, but being stuck between the rock and the
proverbial hard place was a position he'd wedged himself
into. And he wasn't going to be able to come out any time
soon.

How the hell was he supposed to know he'd start actually wanting more from Lily? He hadn't planned on a baby,
hadn't planned on Lily being a permanent fixture in his life.
Of course now she'd be part of his life no matter what, but
beyond the baby, he wanted more.

Nash scooped up the cheesy, veggie-filled omelet and
slid it onto the plate. After pouring a tall glass of juice, he
headed toward the bedroom where he'd left Lily sleeping.

Gripping the plate and glass, Nash turned into the bedroom and froze in the doorway at the seductive sight before
him. Those creamy shoulders against his dark sheets had
his body responded instantly. He never had a woman pull
so many emotions from him, have him so tangled in knots
and have him questioning every motive he had for further-
ing his career.

But Lily had a power over him that scared him to death,
because once she uncovered all of his secrets—and there
were many—she'd never want to see him again. Now that
he'd realized he wanted more from her, he also had another
revelation—Lily would end up hurt in the end and because
he was slowly opening to her, he would be destroyed, as well.

He had nobody to blame but himself.

Being cut from her life, from their child's life was not an
option. She may hate men who used money and power to
get what they wanted, but he wouldn't back down, not when
his child was the central point.

Nash moved into the room, setting the plate and glass on the nightstand. Easing down onto the bed, Nash rested his hip next to hers. Those sheets had never looked better, gliding over and across Lily's curves and silky skin, making her look like a pinup model.

The urge to peel down those covers and reveal her natural beauty overwhelmed him. He'd gotten her from the trailer to his rental home. He was easing her into his life slowly. The ache to be closer to her exploded inside him. He had to touch her, had to feel that delicate skin beneath his rough hands.

Nash's fingertips trailed over Lily's bare arm, leaving goose bumps in the path. Even in sleep she was so responsive to his touch.

Lily stirred, her head shifting toward him, strands of dark hair sliding across her shoulder, and her lids fluttered open. For the briefest of seconds a smile spread across her face before she threw back the covers and sprinted to the adjoining bath.

Morning sickness. Nash hated that there wasn't a damn thing he could do to make her feel better.

He pushed off the bed and padded barefoot across the hardwood floor toward the bathroom. He reached into the cabinet beside the vanity, grabbed a cloth and wet it with cold water before turning to her. He may not be able to stop her misery, but he could at least try to offer support.

Nash pulled her hair back, reaching around to place the cold cloth on her forehead. Hopefully that would help the nausea.

"Go away, Nash," she muttered as she tried to take her hair from his grip. "I don't want you here."

Too damn bad. He wasn't leaving.

After a few more minutes, Lily started to rise and Nash slid his arm around her waist and pulled her up. Limp, she fell back against his chest, resting her head on his shoulder. The way her body fitted against his always felt so right, so perfect. Would he ever be ready to let her go?

"I'm sorry," she murmured. "This is not a side of me I wanted you to see."

Splaying his hand across her abdomen, Nash kissed her temple. "Don't hide from me, Lily."

She covered his hand with her own. "I just wish I knew what we were doing. Where we were going."

That made two of them. For now they had a baby to focus on and the passion that was all-consuming whenever they were close to each other. They may not have the ideal setup or even an idea of what to do next, but they had something.

"I'm not going anywhere," he assured her. "And you're going back to bed. You need to keep up your strength and I made you breakfast."

Lily groaned. "I can't eat. The thought of food makes my stomach turn."

"You'll make yourself even sicker if you don't get something in you."

Without a warning, he bent down, snaked an arm behind her knees and another supported her back as he scooped her up and carried her back into bed.

"You're really taking this role of caring for me to the extreme." She slid her arms around his neck and closed her eyes. "But I'm too tired to argue. When I feel better in a couple hours we'll discuss this caveman persona you've taken on."

Smiling, Nash eased down onto the rumpled bed. "I'll take the eggs away if you think you can't eat, but at least drink."

Nash took the plate into the kitchen and dumped the contents into the trash. By the time he got back to her, she was propped up against the headboard, sheet pulled up and tucked beneath her arms. The glass of juice was about a quarter of the way gone.

And she was holding his gold designer watch in her hand.

Her eyes sought his across the room. "This is a pretty nice watch," she told him, setting it back down on the nightstand.

Damn it. He'd completely forgotten he'd left that out.

"Thanks. It was a gift."

Not a lie. One of his own jockeys had bought that for him several years ago after a big win.

"For a groom you have a pretty impressive house, too," she said, settling deeper into the pillows. "You must be really good at managing money."

He knew she wasn't fishing, but he also knew he was treading a thin line here. He had to open up about some things or she'd really start to wonder if he was hiding things from her.

Stepping farther into the room, he shrugged. "I don't really have anything to spend my money on. I'm not married, I don't travel or buy lavish things. I work, I come home."

Okay, that last part was a complete lie. But he really was a good manager of money. Because he came from nothing, watching every dollar was deeply instilled into him at a young age.

"How you feeling now?" he asked, desperate to switch topics.

"Good. You know, I do plan on getting up, showering and possibly doing something today." She took another sip of juice before focusing on him as he sank down on the edge of the bed beside her. "Just want you to be aware that I don't plan on sitting on my butt for the next seven months."

"I'll take you anywhere you want to go."

Lily sighed. "I'd like to go into town. There were some cute little boutiques I saw when we were filming, but if I go, I'll be recognized."

Nash rested his hand on her sheet-covered thigh. "If you want to go somewhere, I'll get you there and you won't be bothered."

Quirking a brow, Lily sat her near-empty juice glass on the nightstand. "And how will you do that? Because I'd love to be able to shop for just an hour."

Keeping his plan of action to himself, Nash shot her a grin. "Consider it done."

With the slightest tilt of her head, Lily narrowed her eyes. "You're planning something."

Easing forward, Nash ran a fingertip down her cheek, her neck and to the swell of her breast. "I am. But your job is to feel better, take your time getting ready and just let me know when you're done. I have nothing to do today but be at your service."

Her wide eyes slid over his bare chest, a smile danced around unpainted lips. "Sounds like I better rest up for an eventful day."

Because his body still hadn't gotten the memo that he needed to chill, Nash came to his feet. "I'm going to clean up in the kitchen. Yell if you need anything."

He cursed himself all the way down the hall. Lust, sex, it was always there, hovering between them. She was pregnant with his child, which was a hell of a turn-on, but this wasn't the time to worry about how soon he could have her again. He had to find a way to lessen this instant, physical pull between them. They'd indulged in an affair for months and where had that gotten them?

Too much was at stake, too many lives hinged on his next move.

He needed to touch base with his assistant, needed to send a final offer to Damon Barrington because Nash refused to settle for anything less than he came here for. He had an agenda and he had to stick with it or he'd lose it all.

She had no clue how he did it, she really didn't care.

Lily strolled out of the last boutique with bags in hand and headed toward Nash's truck parked in the back alley. He'd gone in with her, even helped her shop and offered pretty good advice when she would try on things.

Who was this guy? She'd never met a man who actually added input on a woman's purchases. He didn't sit out in his truck, he didn't ask her if she was almost done and he didn't act bored even one time. In fact, in one store he found a blue dress which he threw over the dressing room door, telling her it would look great on her.

Guess what? He'd been right. Not only that, the dress was stretchy and flowy. Perfect for that waistline that would be disappearing in the very near future.

Still, she was trying to put a label on him and so far there were just too many layers. No way could such an intriguing man be narrowed down to just one appealing trait. She could only assume his eye for fashion, his nurturing side and his patience came from being raised by a single mother.

And it was his take-charge, powerful side that must have stemmed from wanting to care for his mother. How could she fault that? How could she even think he was anything like her stepfather? Control was one thing, being protective was another.

Nash pulled the passenger side door open, took her bags and placed them in the extended cab part of the truck before offering his hand and helping her up into the seat.

Lily smiled, her eyes level with his now. "Such a gentleman."

"My mama raised me right," he told her, grabbing the seat belt and reaching across her to fasten it. His hands lingered over her breasts as he adjusted the strap. "Better keep you safe."

"Well, my boobs are fine so you can stop," she laughed. "I take back my gentleman compliment since you just wanted to cop a feel."

Nash's flirty smile had her heart clenching tighter. "You wouldn't want some stuffy gentleman. You like the way I can make you lose control."

Standing in the open truck door, Nash's hand traveled over her leg to slide up under her cotton skirt. "Boring and mundane isn't for you."

Not at all. She always thought she wanted someone who was down-to-earth, more trustworthy than the jerk who exploited her innocence years ago. She never thought she'd find someone who was so laid-back, loyal and had the ability to set her body on fire with such simple gestures. Finding the complete package had never crossed her mind.

When she'd started the affair, she'd definitely gone for appealing. Now she was discovering there was so much more than she'd ever bargained for when it came to Nash.

Lily's breath hitched as Nash's fingers danced across her center. Instantly she parted her legs without even thinking. His mouth, just a breath away from hers, had her aching for that promise of a kiss. Never had she desired or craved a man with such intensity.

"Did you have fun today?" he asked, his hand still moving over her silk panties.

"Yes," she whispered. "What are you doing?"

His eyes darted down to where she was fisting her skirt with both hands. "Getting you ready."

"For what?"

Nash nipped at her lips before breathlessly moving across her cheek to whisper in her ear, "Everything I've ever wanted."

His confident declaration had her shivering. Her head fell back against the seat as her lids closed. This man was beyond potent, beyond sexy and quickly becoming a drug she couldn't be without.

Seconds later he removed his hand, smoothed down her skirt and captured her mouth with his. Lily barely had time to grip his arms before he eased back, his forehead resting against hers.

"You think I'm everything you've ever wanted?" she asked, worried what he'd say, but unable to keep the question inside.

"I think you're everything I didn't know I was looking for and more than I deserve."

Slowly, Nash stepped back, closed the door and rounded the hood.

Well, that was intense. Now she was achy, confused and had questions swirling around in her mind. There was no doubt he could turn her on with whispered words, the tilt of his head with that heavy-lidded stare or a feather-light touch. But she wanted more. The man obviously cared about her or he wouldn't have gone to so much trouble to get her in his home, get her out of the house without being seen by too many people and care for her while she'd been sick.

He didn't have to do all of that, yet he did, never once asking for anything in return.

Added to that, he'd just hinted at his deeper emotions and she had a feeling he had shocked himself with his declaration, if his quick retreat was any indication.

Lily wanted to uncover so much more because she honestly didn't know a whole lot about the man who would be in her life forever—one way or another.

As he maneuvered the truck toward his home, Lily adjusted the air vents. Summer was in full force and the sun beat right in through the windshield, making her even hotter.

As much as her body ached for his, she needed backstory, needed to know what made this impossible-to-resist man so captivating. While they were driving, this was the perfect opportunity to dig in to his life a bit more.

"Where did you grow up?" she asked, breaking the silence.

His hand tightened on the steering wheel. "Not too far from here."

"Have you always worked with horses?"

"Yes."

He wasn't as talkative as she'd hoped, but most men weren't. Still, he never seemed to open up about his past... which made her want to uncover all he held back.

"So you had horses growing up?"

His eyes darted toward her, then back to the road. "We couldn't afford them."

Lily laced her fingers together in her lap and turned to stare out the window as he turned onto his road. "Sorry if I'm prying. I just want to learn more about you."

"Nothing to be sorry about," he told her. "My mom worked for a farm so I was always around horses. We just didn't own any. I always swore I'd have a farm of my own one day."

He had a vision, dreams. He worked hard and didn't sit back and feel sorry for himself about what was missing from his life.

How could she not be intrigued by this man who was so opposite from any other man who'd captured her attention? Everything about Nash was different. There wasn't a doubt in her mind that he held on to his past because he was embarrassed. He was a groom, she was a movie star, but couldn't he see that she saw them as equals?

She'd had very humble beginnings and she'd tried to express how money meant nothing to her. All she wanted was a man she could trust and rely on. The fact Nash turned her inside out with his seduction was just icing on the proverbial cake.

When Nash pulled to a stop in front of his house, Lily hopped out and grabbed some bags while Nash took the others and headed up the porch to unlock the door. Once they were settled inside and the bags were dropped onto the floor inside the foyer, Lily turned to Nash.

"Do you mind if we talk?"

Tossing his keys onto the small table, he turned back to meet her gaze. "I'd hoped we'd be doing other activities. What do you want to talk about?"

Lily stepped forward and reached up to wrap her arms around his neck. Instantly his strong arms enveloped her, always making her feel safe, protected…loved. Could he love her? Was he even thinking along those lines?

"Anything," she said. "I just feel like all we do is get naked and I think we really have so much to discuss. The future, what we're doing, the baby. I still don't know much about you."

Nash pulled back, literally and figuratively, as he stepped around her and let out a sigh. "You know all you need to right now."

Lily turned and followed him into the living room, refusing to accept his evasive tactics. "I know you grew up around horses and that you are close with your mother. That's all."

Across the room, Nash rested his hands on the mantel, his head dropped as tension crackled in the silence between them. Something weighed heavily on those wide shoulders of his, something he didn't want her to know.

Was he worried she'd think less of him? Did he wonder how much he should share just because they had different pasts?

Dread settled deep in the pit of her stomach. Was he hiding something worse? Endless possibilities flooded her mind.

"Nash, I know you're keeping something from me." She eased farther into the room, skirting around the sofa and coming to stand just behind him. "You're scaring me with the silence. It can't be that bad, can it?"

She hoped not. Had her judgment been so off again? *Please, no. Please let it be something that is in actuality very, very minor.*

"You deserve the truth," he muttered, still gripping onto the mantel so tightly his knuckles were white. "This is harder than I thought."

Lily slid a hand over her stomach. What had she done? She stepped back until her hip hit the edge of the sofa arm. She gripped the back of the cushion for support.

What bomb was he about to drop and how would this affect the life of her and her child?

Nash turnèd, his eyes full of vulnerability and fear. Raking a hand through his hair, he met her gaze across the room. "Damon Barrington is my father."

Seven

She'd been played for a fool...again.

Her shaky legs threatened to give out. How could she be so foolish? Was she so blinded by men with pretty words and charming attitudes that she couldn't pick out the liars?

Damon Barrington, billionaire horse racing icon, was Nash's father? Her eyes sought his across the room. He hadn't moved, had hardly blinked as he watched her to gauge her reaction. So many thoughts swirled around in her mind she didn't know how she was supposed to react.

"You lied to me."

That was the bottom line.

Oh, no. Nash's father was a wealthy mogul and famous in his own right in the horse racing industry. How would the media spin this story once word got out who her baby's father was?

The muscle in his jaw ticked as he crossed those muscular arms over his chest. "Yes, I lied."

No defense? Was he just going to reveal that jaw-dropping fact and not elaborate?

Lily rubbed her forehead, hoping to chase away the impending headache. She wouldn't beg him to let her in. He either wanted to tell her or he didn't, but he better have a damn good reason for lying to her face.

"I honestly didn't want to lie to you," he defended, as if her silence had triggered him to speak up for himself.

A laugh escaped her. "And yet you did it anyway."

"Damon doesn't know who I am." In two long strides, Nash closed the gap to stand directly in front of her. Those bright blue eyes held hers as if pleading for her to hear him out. "To my knowledge he never even knew my mother was pregnant. I only found out he was my birth father several months ago and that's when I came to work for him. I needed to see what kind of man he was, needed to know if I even wanted to pursue a relationship with him."

A bit of her heart melted, but he'd still withheld information from her, pretending to be someone he wasn't.

"You're the son of the most prominent man in this industry and you didn't even think to tell me?"

Nash reached for her hands, held them tight against his chest as he took another step toward her. "When we first started our connection was just physical. You know that. But then I started getting more involved with you and I worried about disclosing the truth, but I also knew you'd be leaving at the end of the shoot. I wasn't going to say anything to Damon until you were gone and it never would've affected you. But now…"

Realization dawned on her. He'd had to tell her. But the fact of the matter was he only did so when forced to, and that hurt her more than she cared to admit.

"The baby."

Nash nodded, squeezing her hands as if he was afraid she would turn and run. "I truly never wanted you involved in my mess, in this lie, but things were out of my control."

Lily raised her brows. "Out of your control?"

"Fine." The corners of his mouth lifted slightly, showcasing that devastating smile. "I couldn't control myself around you, but I could control how much of my life I let you in on. I wasn't able to tell you before."

"Why now?" she asked, searching his face, finding only vulnerability masked by a handsome, rugged exterior. "You could've kept this to yourself until you talked to Damon."

He held her hands against his heart with one palm and slid his other hand up along her cheek, his fingers threading through her hair.

"No, I couldn't. You've come to mean more, we mean more, than I thought possible. I wasn't ready for you, Lily. I've had this secret living in me, I couldn't just let anyone in."

His heart beat heavily against her hand and Lily knew that him baring his soul was courageous and brave. He could've kept lying to her, he could've gone to Damon first with this bombshell, but he'd opened himself up.

"Besides," he went on, drawing her closer. "I need you. More than I want to admit, and on a level that terrifies me. No matter what's going on around me, in spite of all my issues, I need the passion we possess. I need you, Lily."

Mercy, when he said things like that her entire body shivered, her stomach flopped as nerves settled deep inside her. He wasn't lying now. No man had ever looked at her the way he did. She saw the raw truth in his eyes. Saw how hard it was to expose himself.

"I need you with me right now," he told her, nipping at her lips. "I need to draw from your strength."

The man was twice her size, with his broad, muscular shoulders, his towering height, yet he wanted her strength? He humbled her with his direct, bold declaration.

"Are you going to tell him soon?" she asked, gripping his shirt.

"I really don't know. Part of me wants to, especially now that the film is done, the racing season is over and the girls aren't under as much pressure."

Lily smiled, warming to the idea of Nash being part of such an amazing family. "You have sisters. Nash, this is such a big deal. You have to go to them. They deserve to know. If you want me to go with you, I will. I'll stay back, too. Whatever you want."

Encircling her waist with both arms, Nash pulled her close where her hands were trapped between them. "I'll go soon. But right now, I want to embrace the fact the mother of my child is in my house where there are no interruptions, no schedules to keep. You're supposed to be relaxing and I have the perfect spot."

She eased back, looking him in the eyes. "Don't keep the truth from me again. We're in this together and I can't be with someone I don't trust."

Those bright eyes held hers, the muscle in his jaw clenched and for a second she thought he was about to say something, but he simply nodded.

"Was that our first fight?" she asked.

Nash nuzzled his lips against her neck, his beard tickling her sensitive skin. "I guess so. We better go kiss and make up."

He walked her backward and Lily couldn't help but laugh as she found herself being drawn more and more into his world. Yes, he'd kept something monumental from her, but in his defense he was still working through the new information himself. She couldn't imagine finding your father at this stage in life and she couldn't blame Nash for being confused on how to respond and what steps to take. This was all new territory and they had to wade through it together.

They headed down the hall, his hands cupping her bottom as he led her into the bedroom.

"This is where you'll stay while you're here," he told her as he trailed his lips across her jawline and to her ear. "Clothing is optional."

A thrill shot through her. Being claimed shouldn't be so arousing, yet she found herself wanting Nash more and more each time he threw down that dominance gauntlet.

With a kick of his foot, the bedroom door slammed shut.

* * *

Nash jerked another bale of hay from the stack and moved it into the stable. Frustration and guilt fueled each aggressive movement. He'd lied to Lily, was still lying to her and had worked his way back into a corner he may never find the way out of.

He'd never forget the look on her face when she'd discovered he was Damon's son. But she only knew part of the truth. The rest of his secret wouldn't be so easily defended and the damn last thing he'd ever intended on doing was hurting her.

His plan was to reveal himself to Damon, figure out how the hell to get those horses and get back to his own estate. He was done living these lies, done hurting people he had been around for the past few months.

As much as the guilt ate at him, he still wouldn't leave without what he came for. Otherwise this whole journey would be in vain.

Sweat poured down his back as he stacked the last bale against the far wall. He'd called and checked on Lily several times today and each time she assured him she was fine and if she needed anything she'd call him. Still, he couldn't help but worry. Would he be like this the entire pregnancy? Always worrying?

Nash knew it wasn't just the pregnancy. Everything was closing in on him at once. He needed to confess now that the racing season was over and Cassie and Tessa were focusing on Cassie's new school. He couldn't wait for Damon to sell those horses to someone else.

Nash's assistant should've already proposed the next offer, now Nash just had to wait.

Waiting was about the dead last thing he wanted to do, but he hadn't gotten this far in life by being impulsive. Timing was everything in reaching your goals.

And timing would definitely play a major role in the next steps he took with Lily. It was like walking through a minefield. One wrong move and every plan, every unexpected blessing could all blow up in his face.

He'd spoken with his mother this morning and she was still worried about him exposing the truth, but Nash assured her he wasn't going to disclose everything, only that Damon was his father. Everything else…hell, he had no clue when to drop that bomb. Would Damon look closer and see the man who had been his rival for so long? They'd not been face-to-face in the business world in years and Nash knew he'd changed. Besides the hair, the beard and the clothes, Nash had done more grunt work on his own land, bulking him up quite a bit and changing his physique.

"You may be the hardest working groom I've ever employed."

Nash jerked around to see Damon striding through the stables. Fate had just presented him with the perfect opportunity…but was he ready to take it?

Damn it, this was harder than he thought. Before him stood the man who was his biological father and had no clue. How would he react? Would putting the fact out in the open change Damon's life? Would he care? Would he embrace Nash as part of the family?

In the past several months since learning the truth, Nash had played this scenario in his head a million times. Now that the perfect opportunity had presented itself, he didn't know how to lead into the life-altering conversation.

"Haven't seen you down here much lately," Nash finally said as he tugged off his work gloves and shoved them in his back pocket.

"The girls are done training, so that's freed up my time." The elderly man rested his hand on one of the gates to a stall, curling his fingers around the wrought-iron bars. "I come down more in the evening now. Been spending some of my days playing with sweet Emily."

Nash smiled. Emily was Damon's granddaughter…and Nash's niece. So many instant family members. Actually, with Ian marrying Cassie, that would make Lily's agent Nash's soon-to-be brother-in-law.

His head was spinning. Everything would start unraveling the moment he told Damon the truth, or the part of the truth that Lily knew.

Nash had no clue how Damon would react to having a long lost son, but he knew damn sure how he'd react if he found out the rest of Nash's identity. Epic anger like nothing Nash had ever seen, of that he was positive.

One step at a time.

"You going to be home later?" Nash asked, resting his hands on his hips.

Horses shuffled in the background, one neighed as if trying to chime into the conversation. Nash was starting to love these stables as much as his own. Damn it, he hadn't counted on getting emotionally invested in this place, this family...Lily.

What the hell was happening to him?

"Should be."

"Mind if I come back around seven? I need a private meeting with you."

Damon's silver brows drew together. "You're not quitting on me, are you, son?"

Son. The word was a generic term yet Damon had no clue just how swiftly he'd hit that nail on the head.

"No, sir."

"You've got me intrigued." Damon let out a robust laugh and nodded. "Sure. Come on up to the house about seven."

"Will Cassie and Tessa be around? They may want to be there, too."

He'd made a split-second decision to include his half-sisters. Honestly, Nash wasn't sure if Damon would want the girls to know, but Nash needed them to. The more time he'd spent here, the more he'd gotten involved in their lives and wanted a chance for a family.

"I can ask," Damon informed him. "You've certainly piqued my curiosity, so I'm sure they'll be intrigued, as well."

Nash swiped his forearm across his sweaty forehead, then rested his hands on his hips. "Great. I'll be up to the main house around seven."

If Lily wanted to join him, he wouldn't turn down her support. He needed her, and that wasn't weakness talking, either.

Besides, if he shared everything he could with her now, perhaps the blow that would inevitably come later wouldn't be so harsh. The only other woman he'd let close to him was his mother. Women in his life had come and gone, nobody really fit. Lily fit...as much as she could with all the jagged edges of his life he'd yet to smooth out.

Nash knew he had fallen into a hole so deep, there was no way out and he was starting to wish for things that could never be.

Eight

Lily resisted the urge to throw her phone, and she would pull the childish tantrum if she didn't have to go through the annoyance of getting a new one.

But she wasn't one to waste money.

For pity's sake, she was so sick of certain people in the industry—ahem, producers, actors, etc.—assuming that because they were a big name, she would jump at the chance to work with them. Then when she declined, the offer of more money really set her teeth to grinding. She couldn't be bought, something they found hard to believe.

Thankfully her agent, Ian, had called with the movie options and the ridiculous counteroffers. He was still trying to find her a film that could accommodate her expanding belly, but Lily wasn't sure how work would fit into the life she was envisioning with Nash. The baby was no problem. A relationship with Nash? How would he feel about Hollywood? There was no way she could stay away from the limelight and she knew he was a private man. He'd made no definite declarations to her, yet she found herself hoping everything would work out, because she truly wanted this amazing man in her life, and not just for the baby.

Swinging her legs around, she propped her feet up on the

leather sofa and settled back against the cushioned armrest. This relaxing nonsense was getting really old really fast and she had only been here a few days. If this lasted her entire pregnancy she would go insane.

Added to that, Nash was very attentive to her needs. Okay, wait, that wasn't a bad thing at all. But the man wouldn't let her do anything for herself. He insisted she take it easy and rest until her next appointment when the doctor would come and assess her.

Funny, Lily didn't recall agreeing to stay with him that long. Apparently he'd assumed she would just live here. That was definitely a talk they would be having soon. At some point she'd have to leave, to pack her things and go back to her life. She didn't want all of this uncertainty in her future.

And she was still reeling from the news that Nash was Damon Barrington's son. Even though her first gut reaction was anger, she had to give Nash the benefit of the doubt. The man was obviously torn. He was struggling with this new identity and working as a groom to get close to his biological father. How could she hold that against him?

He hadn't deliberately lied to her and she'd seen the turmoil he'd battled with over revealing the truth to her. What had he done before coming to the Barringtons' estate? Had he been a groom elsewhere? She assumed he worked with horses since he'd told her he did that as a child. Obviously love for the animals and hard work were in his blood.

Had she been in his shoes, she wouldn't have disclosed her secret to a virtual stranger, either.

Oh, how fate had other plans for them. Lily never would've dreamed she'd be living in Nash's cottage, pregnant with his child while he debated on when and how to drop the paternity bomb on the racing mogul.

The sooner the past came out, the better. Wasn't that true for any type of potential relationship?

The front door opened and closed seconds before Nash's heavy footfalls moved through the foyer. He rounded the arched doorway into the living room and offered her a half smile.

"You look like I feel." She rested an arm along the back of the couch, taking in his lean form as he propped a shoulder against the door frame. "Bad day?"

"I'm grabbing a shower and heading back to the estate." Nash ran a hand along his short beard, around to the back of his neck as he let out a sigh. "I'm going to tell him."

Lily jerked up, gripping the back of the couch. "Does he know you're coming back?"

"Yeah."

Lily couldn't believe he was ready to take this step. She knew he wanted to, but she had no idea he was doing it so soon after telling her. Had opening up to her released something else in him? Something that made him want to get his life in order before the baby came? And, dare she hope, for them to move forward together?

"Do you want me to come?"

Nash's eyes met her, his toe-curling smile spread across his face. "I would, but only if you're comfortable going."

Lily came to her feet, smoothing her simple cotton dress down her legs. Rounding the couch, she crossed the cozy living room. Encircling his neck with her arms, Lily answered his devastating smile with her own.

"I don't want to assume anything in any part of your life, Nash. I know our relationship has been a whirlwind, but I don't think you should go through this alone."

"Damn, I want to hold you," he told her, resting his forehead against hers. "But I smell like the ass end of that stable and I need a shower."

Lily laughed as she settled a quick peck on his lips. "I don't mind, you know. But, go shower. I'll throw on my shoes and pull my hair back real quick."

Nash's brows rose. "That's all you're going to do?"

"Uh, yeah, why?" Stepping back and narrowing her gaze, she crossed her arms. "Are you saying I need to change or put makeup on? I know you're used to seeing me all made up on set, but this is the real me, Nash. No fuss and kind of boring."

His hand snaked out, wrapped around her arm and tugged her until she fell against his chest. "I'm a much bigger fan of the no-fuss Lily. I'm just still surprised that you don't care about getting all made up to leave the house."

With a shrug, she laid her palms against his taut T-shirt. "I'm not like most women and I'm definitely not like most Hollywood women. I'm pretty low-key when I'm not working."

Nash's hands roamed down to cup her bottom as he pulled her hips against his. "That's a good thing. Now let me get in the shower and stop manhandling me or we'll be late."

Rolling her eyes, Lily laughed as he kept squeezing her backside. "Yes, of course. What was I thinking?"

As he moved down the hallway, Lily watched him go. The confident stride, the wide shoulders pulling the material of his sweat-soaked T was beyond sexy and his sense of humor only added to his appeal. She found they were growing more and more comfortable with each other outside the bedroom, not that their passion had diminished any, either.

Within thirty minutes they were in Nash's truck, making the ten-minute drive to the Barrington estate. Lily was nervous for him, but he seemed pretty relaxed with his wrist dangling over the steering wheel, his other hand lightly holding on to hers in her lap.

"So what happened with you today?" he asked, breaking the silence. "Are you feeling bad?"

"No, nothing like that." She glanced out the side window, taking in the beautiful farms with the acres of white fencing as far as the eye could see. "I've been on the phone off and on with Ian. He's still trying to find a part for me that will work with this pregnancy. There was one role that would have been a good fit, but I just turned it down before you got home."

"Turned it down? Why?"

"I'm not ready to commit to something long-term just now." She turned to face him, loving the comfortable feel of his hand wrapped around hers, loving even more how fast they were venturing beyond their physical connection. "Besides, the producer is beyond arrogant and he assumed I'd jump at the script. To be honest, if this was another time, with no complications, I would've sucked it up and taken the film."

"Then take it," he told her simply. "Don't let anything hold you back. If they want you, they'll work around the baby."

"I know they will." She wasn't so sure they would work around the fact that she was falling in love and had no clue where she would end up if Nash wanted a future. "It felt good to say no, though. Money is a big part of negotiating contracts, but he just flashes it like it's the red flag and we're the bull charging in after it."

Perhaps that sounded petty, but she wasn't one to be swayed so easily.

"I just have issues with people throwing money around, thinking that will buy them happiness or anything else they want," she went on. "My stepfather kind of ruined me for the rich type. That sounds strange coming from me with what I pull in per film, but I've never thrown my money around and I certainly have never tried to buy someone to get my way."

Nash tensed. "Not everybody with a lot of money is bad and sometimes they have good intentions but things can still go wrong."

Lily wasn't quite sure how to respond and she was quite frankly shocked that Nash was defending the upper class. But it wasn't worth arguing about and she held tightly to his hand as they pulled into the Barringtons' entrance. The wrought-iron gates, with a scrolling *B* on each side, were standing wide-open, inviting them in.

The long, picturesque drive leading back to the property, showcased the horses out in the pasture and led the way to the grand stone stable up ahead. Of course the family famous for their world-renowned success in the horse racing industry would have something that monumental in their lives front and center.

The months she'd spent filming on this farm and in the surrounding area were some of the best of her life. The small-town atmosphere, the intimate setting and getting to know the family of the story she was depicting was icing on the cake. She'd really grown close to Cassie, Tessa and Damon, and even their cook, Linda. The Barringtons might be small in numbers, but they made up for it in love and determination. Lily wanted that kind of family bond, craved it actually.

Her hand went to her flat stomach and she couldn't help but think ahead to the future about what life would be like with a child...and if the man beside her would be part of it.

"You sure you're ready to do this?" she asked when he pulled up in the circular drive and stopped near the front entrance.

Nash pulled their joined hands up to his lips, kissed the back of hers and gave her a big squeeze. "More than ready."

"What reason will you give them that I'm still here?"

Nash shrugged. "What do you want me to say?"

Lily prided herself on the truth, but she still wasn't ready to disclose her pregnancy to the world, yet. She also didn't want this to be about her or the baby at all. This was Nash's moment to possibly connect with a family he hadn't known existed.

And she was still unsure if she would be part of his family once they really sat down and talked about the future.

One monumental moment at a time.

"We can just tell them we met when I first started filming and became friends and I decided to hang around for a while and take a mini-vacation since the shoot was done."

Nash shot her his signature naughty grin. That sexy smile never failed to arouse her because she knew firsthand what that smile looked like as he rose above her just before he joined their bodies.

"I'm pretty sure they'll know we're more than friends," he told her.

"That's fine," she said with a shrug, realizing she truly didn't care.

She trusted this family to keep things private. They understood the way the media worked, considering they were celebrities in their own right with the Barrington sisters making history with their wins. Besides, she'd come to consider them friends and if she wanted to pursue something more with Nash, she needed to get used to opening herself to those that could quite possibly be a big part of his life.

"I'm just not adding any more information than that and I'm not bringing up the pregnancy. Besides, when you tell them the news, I'll be all but forgotten."

"You could never be forgotten." He smacked a kiss on her hand. "I'm not ready to let our little secret out, either. I like having you and this baby to myself for now."

Nash leaned across the center console, slid a hand along her jawline and captured her lips. Those soft, talented lips had been all over her body, yet when he kissed her with such tenderness and care, she couldn't help but wonder if he held back feelings and emotions he was afraid to express out loud.

Because his silent actions were screaming that he was falling in love with her. Heaven help her, she wanted him to be just as torn as she was. She wanted to know that as she entered into this unknown territory of what she felt could be true love, that she wasn't alone.

"Let's go," he murmured against her lips.

Nine

Nash couldn't let his mind drift to the conversation he had with Lily about her career and he sure as hell couldn't think about how his emotions regarding her were tying him up in knots. He was here for one reason and one reason only—to figure out what Damon Barrington would do with the paternity bomb Nash was about to drop.

"Well, we're all here." Damon smiled, crossing an ankle over his knee in his wingback leather chair in the living room as though he hadn't a care in the world. "I'm anxious to hear what you have to say."

Cassie and Tessa sat on the sofa, their matching bright blue eyes locked on his. Didn't they see it? Hadn't they noticed how they all had the exact same shade of cobalt-blue eyes? He'd purposely not worn contacts when he'd come to the estate, perhaps in hopes that someone would mention his eye color.

Nash sat next to Lily on the other sofa across from Tessa and Cassie. A rich mahogany coffee table sat between them, adorned with a perfect arrangement of summer flowers. The Barrington home was just as lavish and beautiful as his own…a home he was itching to get back to. A home he wanted to show Lily.

The Barrington clan had been surprised to see Lily, but had bought the friend story...or at least they hadn't questioned any further.

Even though Lily wasn't touching him, just her presence beside him was all the support he needed. Lily was his rock right now.

"I've really enjoyed my time working here," he began, fighting off the nerves that threatened to consume him. "I've gotten to know all of you and was able to witness history firsthand when Tessa won the Triple Crown. I celebrated even though I was here and not at the race. Being on the ranch during filming was pretty amazing, too."

"You sure you're not quitting?" Damon chimed in. "This sounds like a lead into a resignation."

Nash shook his head and offered a smile. "I assure you, I'm not quitting."

"Is everything okay?" Cassie asked, her brows drawn in.

The two women on the opposite couch were so similar, yet so different. Both had long, crimson hair and those striking blue eyes, but where Tessa was lean and athletic, Cassie was curvy and softer. Both were beautiful, dynamic women and he realized just how much he wanted to be part of their lives.

Damn it. He'd never let himself be vulnerable before. Business had always ruled his life and in that aspect he kept control gripped in a tight fist. His mother was the only person he'd ever let affect him emotionally. But, in a sense, he was also here for her. It was time the secret came out. She deserved to be free of any guilt or residual turmoil and he deserved to know where he stood in his father's life.

"Everything is fine," Nash assured them. Unable to stay seated another minute, he came to his feet and paced behind the couch. "This is harder than I thought."

Along the mantel sat photos in pewter frames, some pictures were of the girls as children, some of Damon's late wife, Rose, but they all depicted the family and the love they shared.

He'd missed out on all of that. But he couldn't blame his mother. She'd made the choices she thought best under the circumstances. Besides, what's done was done and now he just had to figure out the best way to deal with the facts he had…and still get all he wanted in the end.

"I need to start at the beginning." He turned to face them, rested his hands on his hips. "My mother used to work on this estate years ago. She actually worked here as a trainer before I was born."

Damon's eyes widened. "Other than Cassie, I've only employed one other female trainer."

Nash's heart beat so hard, so fast. He waited, letting the impact truly sink in as he kept his eyes on Damon's.

"Your mother was Elaine James?" Damon asked, almost in a stunned whisper.

Both Cassie and Tessa turned their eyes to their father. Nash waited, wanting to see how the events would unfold before he continued.

"Who's Elaine James?" Tessa asked before glancing back to Nash.

"She was one of the best horse trainers in the industry at one time," Damon told her, still staring at Nash. "I used her during a period when female trainers were frowned upon, but some owners snuck around that. She kept her hair really short, wore a hat and would come in early in the mornings and late at night to work with the horses."

Nash knew all of this, had heard his mom tell that same story over and over of how women were gentler and less competitive by nature so Damon had wanted a woman for the job.

"When my mother left here to take care of her parents, she went to work at another farm several hours away," Nash went on. He forced himself to keep his focus on Damon. Right now, nothing else mattered but gauging the older man's reaction. "It wasn't too long after she'd left that she realized she was pregnant with me."

Damon's gasp nearly echoed in the spacious room. Lily sat quietly with her hands in her lap, but Cassie and Tessa's eyes widened as if they were putting the pieces together.

"This can't be," Damon whispered, his eyes darting around the room frantically, then back to lock on Nash's. "You—"

"I'm your son."

There. He'd admitted half of the truth that had weighed heavily on his shoulders since first arriving here several months ago.

Now what? He honestly hadn't planned this far ahead. He'd definitely planned on the end result, but he hadn't factored in all the uncomfortable moments—and now was one of them.

Stunned silence settled over the room. Lily hadn't moved, she merely sat with her eyes locked on his as if silently sending him support. When his gaze landed on hers, she offered a sweet smile of encouragement.

"Nash, forgive me, but I'm going to need more proof than just your word," Damon finally said. "Where is your mother now?"

Nash came around the couch, taking a seat next to Lily again. Now that the secret was out, or part of it anyway, he could somewhat relax for the moment. But he still kept the upper hand.

"I don't blame you for not taking just my word," Nash told the older man. "My mom had a stroke about six months ago. She's doing much better now, but right after the scare, she confessed that she used to work for you and the two of you were...involved."

Nash refused to elaborate.

"Why didn't she tell me?" Damon asked, his brows drawn in, shoulders stiff. "Once she left, I never heard from her again."

Even through years of rivalry and more recently while

working here in a more personal setting, Nash had never seen Damon so stunned.

"When she left to take on a new role at another farm, she had no idea she was pregnant." Nash rested his elbows on his knees, lacing his fingers together as he looked from his half-sisters to his father. "From what she told me, by the time she found out and got the courage to come back and tell you, she was about eight months pregnant. She worried you wouldn't believe her, or that you would marry her just for the baby and she didn't want you to feel trapped. But she wanted you to know. She said she came back to town and all the buzz was about you and Rose and your recent engagement."

Nash recalled his mother's watery confession when she'd begged him to forgive her for not following through and going to Damon. She'd apologized for keeping Nash from his biological father and said that the years of seeing them as rivals in the industry had nearly killed her.

But how could Nash blame her or be angry? She was young, alone and scared. He sure as hell had no place to judge anyone keeping a secret.

"She told me she didn't want to ruin your relationship with your fiancée," Nash went on. "So she ended up having me and raising me on her own."

The words settled in the air and Nash had to fight to keep from reaching out for Lily's hand. He wanted her familiar touch for support, but more than anything he wanted to re-assure her that their baby would always know her place in a family.

Damon rubbed his forehead as if still processing all this information. "Did she ever marry?"

Was he asking as a man who once cared for Nash's mother or was Damon asking from a father's standpoint, worried about his son having a male role model?

"She did when I was about ten."

"Yet you still have her last name," Damon said, shifting in his seat. "Your stepfather didn't adopt you?"

This was the part of coming clean that was about to get tricky. He had to proceed cautiously because one slip of the tongue and all hell would break loose as the complete truth was finally revealed.

"He did," Nash replied. "I chose to still use my mother's maiden name."

Okay, that was a lie, but Damon couldn't know Nash's true identity...not until Nash was ready to share that fact. And the first person he owed the real truth to was Lily.

Wow, his priorities had definitely shifted since he'd first arrived at Stony Ridge Acres. When the hell did that happen? When did contemplating his next step automatically have his mind shifting to how Lily would react or how Lily would feel?

"So you've been here all this time...spying on us?" Tessa asked, her eyes narrowed as she took both hands and shoved her hair away from her face. "Why not say something right at first? Why the lies?"

Nash cleared his throat. "I wasn't sure I wanted to reveal the truth, to be honest. I've always worked with horses and before I could really make up my mind on how to handle the situation after I learned the truth, the groom position came open. I couldn't pass it up."

"You couldn't have told us who you were before now?" Cassie's eyes were softer, yet still guarded like her sister's.

Yes, he could've, but he'd been busy trying to buy out Damon's prizewinning horses and in his spare time he'd been getting naked with Lily. His priorities had taken a hard turn into unexpected territory.

"I understand this makes an impact on all of your lives," he began, choosing his words carefully. "I had to see if this was even a family that would welcome me, or if I should keep the secret and eventually just leave quietly."

Lily did reach over now and squeezed his hand. The gesture wasn't lost on the Barrington sisters whose eyes darted in their direction.

Nash didn't want to think how that silent action truly spoke volumes for how supportive Lily was and how, right at this moment, his emotions meant more to her than what other people assumed or thought. Damn it. He didn't deserve her loyalty, her kindness and innocence. He was lying to her and no matter how he justified it, no matter how he knew there had been no way around the secrets, he was still in a relationship with a woman who didn't even know his real name.

"And you've deemed us fit to be in your life now?" Tessa came to her feet, tugged the hem of her shirt down and crossed her arms. "I'm skeptical, for sure, but more than anything I'm a little hurt you basically spied on us."

Nash nodded. "I expected all of you to feel that way, but I had to do what was best for me and my mom. My stepfather is gone and I've taken care of her for years. I have to put her wishes and feelings above anything else."

"She was okay with you coming here?" Damon chimed in.

"She left that decision up to me," Nash informed him. "But she was worried that, at this point, I would disrupt your lives."

"I have a brother," Cassie whispered, her eyes filling.

"Cass," Damon warned. "We still need proof, though I'm pretty sure Nash is telling the truth."

"It's the eyes," Cassie said with a wide smile as she swiped her damp cheeks. "He's got our eyes."

Obviously not one to show emotions, Tessa turned to her father. "How could you go from his mother to our mom in such a short period of time?" she asked, throwing her arms wide. She still hadn't sat back down and Nash was pretty sure she really wanted to storm out. She was definitely the more vocal sister.

Damon eased back in his chair, his hands gripping the leather armrests. "Without getting into details you all probably don't want to hear, Elaine and I were attracted to each other, but we never fell in love or even mentioned a relationship beyond the physical. Once she left, I met Rose and love at first sight was something I had believed to be a myth until I saw her. We met one day, went on our first date the next and were inseparable. She was it for me."

Nash swallowed. His mother had pretty much said the same thing. She and Damon hadn't been in love, just young lovers having a good time. And they were from two different worlds, which was probably frowned upon at that time.

The beginning of his mother and Damon's relationship mirrored that of Lily and himself. Only Nash had every intention of a different ending.

"Your eyes," Tessa murmured as she slowly maneuvered around the coffee table and sat on the other side of him. "I knew when you first came here that there was something about you."

Nash nodded, trying not to get too wrapped up in these emotions that threatened to rise to the surface. "I saw it first thing, too."

He hadn't even realized until this moment just how much he wanted the girls and Damon to accept him. He may have more money than he would ever need or know what to do with, but there was one thing money couldn't buy...a family. And deep inside, that's what he'd always wanted.

"You really are my brother?" she asked, her voice cracking.

Nash smiled. "Yeah, I am."

"So what now?"

Nash shifted to focus back on Damon, who still had his silver brows drawn as if he didn't know whether to be confused or angry. This was another part of the plan that he'd have to tread lightly on because as much as Nash wanted to get those horses, he also wanted this family. He just had to figure out a way to cleverly capture it all.

"That's up to you," Nash told his father. "I love working here, but I understand if you aren't able to trust me right now."

"No," Cassie said, shaking her head. "You've proven your-self. Right, Dad? Nash is the hardest working groom we've ever had."

Damon nodded, easing forward in his seat. "You're more than welcome to keep working here, Nash. And, if you own any horses, feel free to house them here."

Oh, the irony. Between the double families, the Barringtons, Lily and his baby, and the horse ownership, Nash was spinning in circles and feared he'd have a hard time keeping all of his lies straight before he could present them in a justifiable manner.

"I actually don't have any right now," he told Damon, which was partially true. Nash's horses just weren't here locally.

"The groom position is yours as long as you want it." Damon came to his feet and Nash assumed that was his cue to do the same. "And if you get a horse, these stables are available to you anytime."

Nash stood before his father, the same man he was try-ing to buy out, and held out his hand. "I appreciate that."

Damon clasped Nash's hand and pulled him into a one-armed man-hug before easing back. The sadness in his eyes matched his tone. "I'm sorry about your mother. If there's anything I can do…"

"Thanks." Absolutely no way would anyone else take care of his mother. Nash was a bit protective of her and right now he wasn't ready to discuss her too much. "She's doing really well, actually."

Damon nodded and released Nash's hand. "You've cer-tainly dropped a bomb I hadn't expected. I hope my stunned silence at times didn't make you feel unwelcome, I'm just still so shocked."

"I understand. I was shocked, too, but I've had several months to process this." Nash glanced down to Lily who was toying with the hem of her dress lying against her tanned thighs. "I think Lily and I will go and let you all talk things over in private."

He extended his hand to Lily and assisted her up. She presented a killer smile to Damon and patted his arm.

"You've really been blessed with this news," she told him. "Shocking as it may be, your family has grown and you've gained a wonderful son."

Damon embraced her and patted her back. "Rose would've loved you."

Nash knew Damon and Lily had bonded pretty well during the filming of Damon's life. Lily had played Damon's late wife and the two had often discussed the late Mrs. Barrington. Damon was all too eager to share stories and memories of his wife.

Guilt and a new set of nerves settled deep in Nash's gut. There was still one more piece of damning information he had to reveal. He'd grown beyond the man who initially settled in here to spy on his rival and to have a heated affair.

Now Nash wanted a family, both families, and he had no choice but to destroy any amount of progress he'd made. Once the truth revealed itself, any hope of having a relationship with the Barringtons or Lily would be gone.

"I just hope once the film is out, people will see how amazing this family truly is, and not just in the racing world." Lily made her way around the room and hugged Tessa and Cassie. "I'll be in town for a while," she informed them. "Perhaps we could go to lunch or something?"

Cassie smiled. "I'd like that. I assume we can find you at Nash's?"

Lily laughed. "Yes, but please don't let that get out."

"We'd never say a word," Tessa assured. "I'm glad you'll be here awhile. Now that Cassie and I have a little more free time, we could use a girls' day out."

Nash watched as the sisters he'd just inherited bonded with the mother of his child.

Failure wasn't an option. Not when he had this much at

stake. All he could do now was wait for his assistant to get back to him on whether or not Damon would take the deal. Until then, Nash was at a standstill and unclear of his next move.

Ten

Insomnia was a cruel, unwelcome friend.

Lily tried her hardest not to make too much noise as she searched the kitchen for her guilty pleasure. Unfortunately, Nash didn't keep cocoa or chocolate syrup on hand.

With the gallon of milk in tow, she closed the refrigerator door and thought how she could get her chocolate milk fix. Being a chocoholic was her downfall, right behind the grilled cheese. Hey, she could have worse addictions. Granted, food obsessions in LA were unheard of, considering women there opted to starve themselves so they were skinnier than their so-called friends. Lily loved food too much for all of that nonsense.

And she had a weakness for chocolate milk.

With a brilliant plan in mind, she jerked open the freezer and instantly spotted a gallon of chocolate swirl ice cream. Perfect backup in a pinch.

Grabbing the largest glass she could reach in the cabinet, Lily found a spoon and scooped a hefty helping of ice cream into her glass before she carefully poured milk over it. She saw nothing wrong with having a chocolate float at two in the morning. One good thing about the pregnancy, she could totally blame her crazy cravings on the baby. Of course, even when she wasn't pregnant she'd wake up in the middle of the night for chocolate milk, but nobody needed to know that.

Using the spoon, she stabbed at the hunk of ice cream at the bottom of the glass in an attempt to break some of it up into chocolaty goodness. She'd just taken her first sip when footsteps shuffled over the tile behind her.

Licking the milk mustache off her top lip, because she was a classy lady, Lily turned to see Nash looking very sexy and sleepy with his lounge pants sitting low on his narrow waist. His long, disheveled hair fell across his forehead and those bright blue eyes zeroed in on the glass in her hand before darting to the ice cream and milk on the counter.

Even with just the small light on over the stove, she could see the amusement overriding the tiredness etched on his face.

"Don't judge me."

She took another gulp and welcomed the coolness as it spread through her body. Who knew being pregnant turned on some sort of internal furnace?

"I don't even know what to say," he told her with a smirk. "Is this something you normally do?"

Lily leaned her hip against the center island. "When I can't sleep I usually get up and have some chocolate milk, but you didn't have any syrup so I had to improvise."

With a slight tilt of his head, his eyes instantly flashed with concern. "What's on your mind that you're not sleeping?"

Clutching her glass, Lily laughed. Where to start? "Everything at the moment."

Remaining in the doorway with his shoulder propped against the jam, Nash crossed his arms over his deliciously bare chest. Would she ever tire of looking at him? Touching him?

The fire that continued to burn between them wasn't all that had her wanting more with this intriguing man. He excited her in ways she'd never felt before, he made her feel as if she was actually meaningful to his life, as if he wasn't only with her for her celebrity status. And he was honest. She needed honesty. Coming from a land where lies flew as quickly as the wind, she needed that stability. She needed him.

Earlier tonight when she'd seen him vulnerable, baring his soul to a family that didn't know he existed had twisted something even deeper within her. There was so much more to Nash than she'd first uncovered and all she knew was she wanted to discover the rest.

"Talk to me," he murmured, that low tone washing over her. "I'm a pretty good listener."

He was good at everything…hence her hang-ups and torments.

"I'm just thinking." *Worrying.* "With Damon knowing who you are now, what will happen next with your life."

She took a drink, thankful for the prop in her hands and the comfort of her guilty pleasure. Having these thoughts occupy her mind was one thing, letting them out in the open was another. But here they were, surrounded by near darkness and silence where they would have no interruptions. Might as well lay out some of her concerns.

"That's not all on your mind."

Lily caught his stare from across the room. He knew her all too well. And here she'd worried they only knew each other intimately. For months everything had been so one-dimensional, which had worked perfectly for them until the shocking baby news. Even after that, though, they'd kept things physical, not delving too deep.

Everything about them had recently shifted. She knew his fears of opening up to Damon and the girls just as he knew her fears of the baby and her career. They were in this together, bonding, growing closer…and that scared her to death.

"I don't want this child to ever worry about where she stands with us." Lily slid her free hand over her stomach, silently vowing protection over her innocent baby. "I saw the torment in your eyes, Nash. I saw the vulnerability when you were talking to Damon. You're a strong man, but family is something that I can see you take very seriously. I guess I'm worried where we're headed, not just you and me, but this baby. I don't want her life torn between ours."

Nash moved farther into the kitchen. The closer he came, the bigger he seemed to get. Those tanned, bare, broad shoulders, wrapped over muscles from working hard on a farm, would make any woman's knees weak and toes curl. She was no exception.

His hand slid over hers on her stomach. "This child will never question how much we love her. No matter where we are, this child takes top priority."

Thrilled that his level of passion for protecting and loving this child was the same as hers, Lily smiled. But she didn't miss the fact he avoided the topic of them as a couple.

One day at a time. She still had months to think things through. Ian was totally understanding in her taking a bit of time off since she'd just wrapped filming and was coming to terms with the pregnancy. She couldn't be happier that she'd taken him on as her agent.

So while he was figuring out her next career move, Lily was trying to get a handle on her personal life and how she could keep her career, raise the baby and figure out her feelings for Nash. Whatever they had went beyond lust, beyond sexual, but she couldn't identify it quite yet.

Without another word, Nash took the cold glass from her hand and took a drink. Milk settled into his mustache before his tongue darted out to swipe it away.

She'd never been attracted to a man with a scruffy beard and unkempt hair before, but something about Nash had been intriguing from the second she'd met him. Lily had actually found his ruggedness sexy and a nice change from all the pretty boys in Hollywood who worried too much about their looks.

"You're right," he told her. "This is good."

Reclaiming her glass, Lily took another drink and made a mental note to go to the store for syrup first thing in the morning. A woman had needs, after all.

Speaking of needs, the way Nash's heavy-lidded eyes raked over her silky chemise made her shiver with arousal. She'd worried about staying with Nash because she'd been afraid all they would do was act on all this sexual chemistry they had instead of figuring things out. But staying with him had forced them to evaluate what was going on between them and open up a little more each day.

The sex was just icing on the proverbial cake.

Without a word, Nash took the glass from her once again, but instead of taking a drink, he set it on the counter. The clank of the glass on the granite echoed in the silence. His strong hands glided over her silky gown at her sides as he eased her closer to him. The warmth of his fingers burned through the thin layer of material.

"I know something else that cures insomnia," he murmured. "It's quite a bit more grown-up than chocolate milk."

With a firm hold around her waist, Nash leaned forward, sliding his lips over her jawline and down her neck. Trembling against his touch, Lily gripped his biceps and tilted her head back as he continued his path on down toward the slope of her sensitive breasts.

Nash cleverly reached up, easing the thin straps of the chemise down with just the brush of his fingertips. Lily lifted her arms, ridding herself of the straps and in a swift whoosh, the flimsy garment puddled at her feet, leaving her wearing nothing but his arousing touch.

Nash quickly took advantage of her state of undress and bent his head to continue his torture with those talented lips. Lily arched into him as he claimed her with only his mouth. While Nash thoroughly loved on her breasts with his hands and lips, she slid her thumbs into the waistband of his pants and shoved them down. A sense of urgency overwhelmed her.

Nash pulled away from her breast and before she could protest, he slammed his mouth onto hers. Wrapping her arms around him, she threaded her fingers through his hair and held him in place. Without breaking contact from her mouth, Nash lifted her off the ground, keeping her flush with his body.

Encircling his waist with her legs, Lily locked her ankles behind his back and clung tighter as he moved from the kitchen toward the hall. Lily clutched at his shoulders, angling her mouth to take the kiss deeper in an attempt to take some control. When he tried to break the kiss, her lips only found his again. She needed his mouth on her, needed that contact with a desire she'd not known before Nash.

He backed her into the wall before they made it to the bedroom door. Grabbing her hands from his shoulders, he plastered them beside her head and held her in place with only his hard, firm body.

"None of that," he whispered against her lips when she tried to capture his mouth again. "You're supposed to be relaxing, which means I'm in control."

Lily smiled, tilted her hips toward him, pleased when his lids shuddered closed as he let out a low groan.

"You would tempt a saint," he growled.

"I only want to tempt you."

Nash's eyes opened, focused on hers as he slid into her. Those cobalt baby blues demanded her attention, held her captivated as he set the pace. Lily couldn't look away if she wanted to.

Everything about Nash was demanding, yet attentive, bold, yet nurturing…in bed and out.

As her hips met his and her hands continued to grip his shoulders, Lily watched Nash's face. A myriad of emotions crossed before her eyes: determination, arousal, need…and love. She saw it as plain as she could feel him. The man loved her, but whether he was ready to admit it to himself was an entirely different matter. He had enough going on right now without professing his love to her.

Still, she couldn't help but feel a bit relieved that he may have developed such strong feelings for her. Because she had already started falling for the simple groom with a complicated life.

Lily continued to hold his gaze as she trembled with release, and as Nash followed suit, he didn't look away. Those bright blues stayed transfixed on her, sending a new wave of shivers coursing through her.

And when their tremors passed, Nash leaned his forehead against hers and whispered, "You're more than I ever thought I was looking for."

Eleven

Nash had no clue what the hell had transpired in the hall just moments ago, but as he lay holding Lily in his arms on the bed they'd shared for a week, he realized two things: one, she was more vulnerable than she wanted him to see; and two, he'd let some of his own feelings slip out when his guard had been let down.

He had to keep his emotions close to his chest. He couldn't afford to reveal just how fast he'd started falling for Lily.

She was right when she'd said family meant everything to him and that's why he had to remain in control. He had to grip tightly with both hands: the Barringtons in one and Lily and his baby in the other.

She shifted against his side, her hand drifted over his abdomen as she slid one smooth leg over his thigh. He'd carried her back to bed after they had frantic sex in the hallway.

Yeah, he was a real classy guy not being able to hold back long enough to take those few extra steps to get her into bed. She didn't seem to mind. Actually if her moans and nails biting into his shoulders had been any indication, she'd rather enjoyed herself.

As frantic and aggressive as they'd been together, something had passed between them…something silent, yet significant. He'd seen so much in her eyes and he worried what she'd seen in his.

Lying in silence for several minutes, Nash knew Lily wasn't going to sleep anytime soon.

"I'm sure you see the parallel in my mother's pregnancy and yours," he told her, breaking the silence. He glided his fingertips along her bare arm across his body. "You're not here because of that. You're here because I want you here."

Lily's body softened against his. "I know. I know we started off as just a private affair and suddenly we're both thrust into a world we have no clue how to face. One day at a time is all we can do right now."

Relieved that she knew that much, Nash wished he could tell her the rest. Wished he could fully disclose his identity. But telling her now would certainly murder any chance he had of being with her. He needed more time.

"But, I do need to make some decisions soon," she said after a minute of silence. "I can't stay in Virginia forever and avoid my responsibilities."

Forever. Was he ready to use such a word when thinking of them in terms of a couple? He'd never considered forever with one woman before, but something about Lily made him reconsider his list of priorities. She made him want to be a better man, not always putting business first and really focusing on life. But he'd already dived headfirst into this plan before he met her and, unfortunately, there was no turning back now.

Damn it. He'd had every intention of coming out of this charade unchanged and besting his rival.

"Have you told your mom about the baby?" he asked.

Her warm breath tickled his side as she blew out a sigh. "Not yet. This isn't something I want to just tell her over the phone. Besides, I'd like to go visit her, anyway. I try to get there between films."

Moonlight filtered through the crack in the curtains, slanting a soft glow across the bed. So many things raced through his mind, from the buying of Damon's horses to the baby, but one thing was certain. He couldn't let Lily go. He kept having images of her in his home, his real home, on his grounds and in his stables. She would fit in perfectly and his staff would be just as charmed by her as he was.

"What do you say we go on a picnic or horseback riding tomorrow…well, today." He stopped, wondering if that was even a possibility. "Are you even allowed to ride horses pregnant?"

She turned, fisted her hand and rested her chin on it. "I'm not sure, really. Are you asking me on a date?" she asked with a smile.

Smoothing her hair away from her face and shoving it behind her shoulders, he trailed a fingertip down her cheek. "Yeah. Kind of working backward, but what do you say?"

"I'd love to go on a date with you. Let's just stick with the picnic for now, okay?"

Why her bright smile and upbeat tone sent his heart into overdrive was beyond him. They were having a baby, they'd been intimate and she went with him to offer support with Damon. Now he decided to ask her on a date?

"If we have a big date planned, I better get some sleep," she told him around a yawn.

"Need more ice cream and milk?" he chuckled.

"Oh, no." Her delicate laugh filled his room, his heart. "Your way worked so much better to cure my insomnia. You wore me out."

Nash couldn't help but smile as he kissed the top of her head. "That's the idea. Now rest."

He pulled the thin comforter up around her shoulders and held her tight until her breathing slowed and her hand beneath his went lax.

Nash couldn't wait for the sun to rise, to get in some time at Stony Ridge, then go on a date with Lily. He needed her to see who he truly was before she found out about the other side to him. He needed her to see that there was so much more to him than his millionaire businessman and million-aire persona. He was still the man who tended to horses and enjoyed the simple ways of life.

But first, he needed to find out where Damon stood on selling those thoroughbreds. Little did Damon know, his newfound son was also his most hated rival in the racing industry.

"You've got to be kidding me."

Lily cupped her hand and scooped up the cool, refreshing water, playfully sending it in Nash's direction.

"Come on," she teased. "You're a country boy. Don't let a little creek water scare you."

After a filling picnic consisting of sandwiches, fresh fruit, lemonade and chocolate chip cookies, Lily had toed off her sandals and stepped into the brisk creek to splash and play around. Nash still lay propped on one elbow on their blanket, watching her with a huge, devastating grin.

"Oh, I'm not scared," he retorted as he sat up and pulled off his cowboy boots and socks. "It's you who should be scared."

Shivers raced across her body at his threat. She slid her toes gently over the creek bed in an attempt to avoid the sharp pebbles.

Nash came to his feet, reached behind his head and yanked his T-shirt off and flung it to the side. Oh, my. Those taut muscles all tanned and perfectly sculpted had her belly quivering. He knew how to fight fire with fire…he poured gasoline on it.

"Keep looking at me like that and I'll clear off that blanket in two seconds and make better use of it," he warned as he stepped closer to the creek.

At the edge, he stopped and rolled up his jeans. Lily propped her hands on her hips, loving this playful, relaxed day. With the sun high in the sky, the warmth of summer was in full swing and the country setting was just what the doctor ordered. Nash had told her about this creek that ran through the back of his rental property. It was simple, private and perfect for them. And from how he kept eyeing her in her short tank-style dress, she figured privacy was going to be to their benefit very shortly.

Would she ever tire of how he watched her? How his eyes seemed to drink her in, in one sweeping glance? Each time she caught him visually sampling her, her need for him sharpened even more.

"Damn, that's cold," he complained as he put one foot in. "You didn't tell me that."

Rolling her eyes, Lily laughed. "It's refreshing. Don't be such a baby."

"I'll show you baby."

He bent down, scooped up handfuls of water and trickled a stream down her bare legs. The coolness did nothing to ease the heat rushing through her. Everything with this man turned intimate and aroused her like nothing else she'd ever experienced.

He made her laugh, made her appreciate how a relationship between two totally opposite people may actually work.

And she found herself wanting that more and more each day. She wanted to be with a man who wasn't afraid to lean on someone else when he needed to, a man who could also protect and take charge without being overbearing. She wanted Nash.

Still bent down, his hands lingered on her legs, those bright eyes came up to hold her gaze. "You're right," he said. "This was a great way to cool off."

"You turn everything into sex," she laughed, even though she wanted him to rip her clothes off and have his way with her on the creek bank.

His hand stilled, that naughty grin widened. "I'm a guy. Of course everything is about sex. It doesn't help you're looking at me like you want to gobble me up."

Lily couldn't help herself. She took her foot and tapped

his chest with just enough force to send him butt first into the water. Crossing her arms, she tried her hardest not to double over with laughter as he glared up at her with a smirk on his face.

"Thought you needed to cool off," she quipped with a shrug.

"Oh, baby, I always need to cool off around you," he told her as he started to come to his feet. Water dripped off his hands, his thighs as he wrapped his wet arms around her and pulled her flush against him. "Don't tell me you don't want me for my body."

Lily's hands were trapped between them, so she laid her palms against his bare chest. "You have a very fine body, Nash. No denying that."

"Gee, you make a guy feel really wanted."

Lily slid her hands up to his shoulders, around his neck and laced her fingers together. "I think your ego needs bringing down a notch sometimes."

Those kissable lips offered up a sideways grin. "And you're the woman to do that?"

"That I am," she said. "I bet you've used this body to get what you wanted from women before. I can't blame you, though, you're a sexy man. All those muscles from manual labor, the scruffy, rugged beard and shaggy hair…you give off a sense of mystery. But I want more than the body, more than the seductive exterior."

She nipped at his lips, loving the sensation of his soft beard feathering over her skin. "I want to uncover the mystery," she whispered against his mouth. "I feel there's so much more to you than what you're showing me."

Nash stiffened in her arms, those bright eyes narrowed in on hers. "Be careful what you wish for," he told her. "What if you don't like what you uncover?"

What started out as playful had taken a turn into an area she wasn't sure about heading into. While she'd been half-joking, his tone implied he was dead serious. Was he implying there was something she wouldn't like about him? Was he hiding something else? Everyone had secrets, but the way he'd issued that warning, Lily couldn't help but wonder what he meant.

"How much more do I need to uncover?" she asked, swallowing the lump of fear in her throat.

Those strong hands on her back slid down to cup her backside. "You could spend a lifetime unraveling me."

Arousal slammed through her, but something else, something akin to love spiraled right along with it. Was he indicating he may want forever? Were they honestly ready for that type of talk?

All of a sudden black dots danced in front of Nash's face as the world tilted. Her heart rate kicked up and her stomach flipped with nerves as she broke out into a sweat.

Lily heard him call her name before her world went black.

Twelve

Cradling Lily in his arms and beating a path through the field and toward his house, Nash said a prayer with each step he took. One second he'd been ready to confess his life to her, the next she'd slumped against his body. A fear like nothing he'd ever known slammed into him.

Never before had Nash been so consumed with worry or gut-wrenching panic. She was pale, too pale. Those pink lips were white and she was deadweight in his arms.

As he reached his patio, Nash laid her down on the cushioned chaise lounge which was thankfully shaded by his house this time of day.

Lily's eyelids fluttered, her face turned toward him and Nash eased down beside her, smoothing her hair back from her face, which was starting to regain some color.

"Nash?"

"It's okay," he assured her, cursing his shaking hands. "You passed out on me. Just lie here for a bit. I'm going to run in the house and get my cell to call the doctor."

Her fingers wrapped around his arm before he could move. "No, please. I'm fine. I think it was just the heat."

"I want the doctor to come and make sure you and the baby are healthy." Uncurling her fingers from his arm, he brought her hand to his lips and kissed her palm. "I need to know."

He didn't wait for her to argue, it wouldn't matter if she did because he was up and in the house in seconds. As he placed the call, he went back out to Lily who was still lying down, now with her arms wrapped around her abdomen.

The doctor assured Nash he would be there within ten minutes. Sometimes money wasn't the root of all evil.

Nash's hand slid over hers. "Are you in pain?"

Shaking her head, Lily squeezed her lids together. A lone tear streaked out, sliding down her temple and into her hair. Nash eased back down beside her, swiping the moisture away.

"Talk to me," he urged, placing his palm against her cheek. "Are you hurting or still dizzy?"

She opened her eyes and stared up at him. "I feel fine. I just got scared. What if something is wrong? I mean, just because I feel fine now doesn't mean something isn't going on inside my body."

He shared her dread, but refused to be anything less than strong for her, for their baby. Had his mother gone through this type of fear and worry? Nash couldn't even fathom his strong, vibrant mother being alone and facing all this uncertainty without support.

"Everything will be fine," he assured her. "The doctor will give you a clean bill of health."

Her dark eyes filled as her chin began to quiver. Damn it, he hated being so helpless. What could he offer her right now but promising words and a shoulder to cry on? Even paying for the best doctor to be at their beck and call couldn't prevent something unexpected from happening.

Nash was used to getting his way, getting what he wanted, whether it be through his power or financial control. But this child and this woman he was coming to deeply care for couldn't be handled in the same manner as his business dealings.

The fact he was putting them above everything else, even his end goal, should tell him he was falling in deeper and deeper with this Hollywood starlet.

"What are we doing?" she asked, her voice trembling. "How can we raise a child when we live on opposite sides of the country and our lives are so different?"

Nash knew enough about pregnancy to know that her hormones were all over the place and with the scare she'd just had, Lily's mind was going into overdrive. Treading carefully with each word was the only way to keep her calm.

"Right now, all we're going to think about is relaxing because our baby is depending on us to keep her safe."

That misty gaze held his. After a moment's hesitation, Lily nodded and smiled. "You're right. As long as she's healthy, we can figure out the rest."

Nash slid her hand between both of his and squeezed. "You know we keep referring to this baby as 'she'?"

Lily's smile widened. "I know. Honestly I don't care what the sex is, but something just tells me this will be a girl."

The image of a baby with Lily's stunning, natural beauty gripped his heart. No matter if the baby had his bright blue eyes or her dark features, Nash knew one thing, this baby would be loved, would know her place in the family and would want for nothing...and he didn't just mean monetary things, either.

After the doctor had come and gone, giving Lily a clean bill of health, Nash had still insisted she lie around and do nothing. Absolutely nothing. This hero act was sweet for about five minutes, but she was really getting tired of him jerking around to see if she was okay with every move she made .

Lily settled deeper into the propped pillows behind her back and crossed her ankles. She probably should warn Nash she didn't plan on staying in this bed the entire time she was here. Tomorrow she would get up and do...something.

Her phone chimed on the nightstand and Lily glanced over to see a text from Ian. She hadn't checked her phone since this morning, considering she'd planned on a more fun-filled day she hadn't wanted to be interrupted. But when the events had turned more worrisome, she'd not even given work a second thought.

Reaching for her phone, she quickly read his text.

Did you get my voice mail?

Lily went to her messages and listened, her heart thumping as she realized Ian was presenting her with a role made for her and she had to make the decision rather quickly. As in, by Monday morning.

After she listened fully to his message, she fired back a text stating she'd listened and she was definitely interested and he would have a decision by tomorrow night. She didn't go into details of her day's events because even though he knew she was expecting, he didn't need to worry she couldn't do her job.

As she was pondering the role and how wonderful the opportunity would be for her, Nash rounded the corner with his phone in hand.

"Still feeling good?" he asked, coming to stand beside the bed.

"I hope you don't think I'm lying in this bed for months," she informed him. "I'm going to have bedsores."

Nash lifted her legs and sat down, placing her feet across his lap. "Yeah, well we had one outing and you went out like a light. I don't think my heart could take too much more of that."

His heart. That was an area they'd yet to explore. She honestly wanted to know what was in his heart where they were concerned.

"I just got off the phone with Damon."

Lily perked up. "Did he call you?"

Nash smiled. "Yeah. He wants us to come out to the estate for lunch tomorrow. You don't have to if you don't want to. Don't feel obligated."

Lily sat straight up. "First of all, that's a little hurtful that you think I wouldn't want to. Second, if you're not comfortable with me around your new family, just say so. I know you're wanting to get to know them and I'm still an outsider."

Nash slid his hands up her legs to her thighs as he gripped her and leaned forward. "I want you there. Never doubt that I want you with me. I didn't want you to feel like I was dragging you through my family drama right now."

"Fair enough." The fact he wanted her there spoke volumes for the direction their relationship was headed. "Are you going to tell them about the baby?"

Nash's thumbs slid back and forth over her bare thighs, making this conversation hard to focus on. But she realized he wasn't even paying attention to the gesture when he sighed and shook his head.

"I'm not sure," he said. "I want to leave that up to you since we're not ready for the media to get wind of it."

"Well, Ian knows, so Cassie may, too. Although he did promise to keep the information to himself."

Lily thought about the Barringtons, about how dynamic this family was and how the media tended to hound them, too. They would understand the need for privacy, especially when an innocent baby was involved. A close-knit family like that knew all about loyalty and protecting those around them.

"I don't mind if we tell them," she said, pleased when his mouth split into a wide grin.

"Seriously?"

"Sure. That will give everyone something positive to discuss, something that takes the edge off the intensity of you shocking them with your identity."

The smile on his face faded, the muscle in his jaw clenched. Something she couldn't identify passed over his eyes.

"You all right?" she asked, wondering what she'd said that had him so worried.

He blinked, and an instant transformation had his smile returning. "I'm good. Just thinking about how I'll fit into Damon's life now, I guess."

Framing his face in her hands, Lily held his gaze. "You'll fit in perfectly. You all already have a love of horses, it's in the blood. Things will all work out, you'll see."

His dark brows drew down as if some worry still plagued him. "I pray you're right."

"That was wonderful," Lily declared as she sat her napkin on the table. "Thank you."

"My pleasure," Damon replied with a smile.

Nash hadn't known what to expect when coming for lunch today, but so far he was pleasantly surprised at how easily he and Lily had slid into the family role…as if they were a real couple coming to his parents' for a gathering.

With Ian, Cassie and Cassie's little girl on one side of the long table and Tessa and her husband, Grant, on the side with Nash and Lily, Damon sat at the head like the grand patriarch he was.

The confident man had no clue he'd just hosted his rival.

Nash wished more than anything he and Damon weren't at odds in the business world. Nash hated lying, hated being someone he wasn't just to get the prizewinning horses to complete his breeding program. He hadn't worried about this when he'd first come onto the scene.

He had Lily to thank for that bout of conscience. When he'd set out to get the inside scoop on Damon's plan after the racing season, Nash had been ready to steal, lie and cheat to get what he wanted. But Lily made him want to be a better man.

Nash had also gotten to know Damon on a more personal level and the elderly man wasn't too different from Nash. They both knew what they wanted, and both went after it full force...how could Nash fault that? Damon wasn't the man Nash had originally thought.

Damon had a passion for the sport, just like Nash. The man cared for his family, would do anything to protect them. Nash hadn't seen that side of him years ago in the circuit. All Nash had known was how ruthless Damon could be. And, honestly, Nash had actually recognized how alike he and his father were.

Trouble now was, Nash was already wrapped so tightly in his own lies. He still wanted those horses, still needed desperately to breed them with his own back on his estate. He'd not had the best seasons lately and he had to do something.

Lily's hand slid over his leg under the table. "You okay?" she whispered.

Pushing away thoughts of business, Nash patted her hand. "Yeah."

"Nash, I'd like to talk with you a moment if you don't mind taking a walk down to the stables with me," Damon said, not really asking. A man like Damon Barrington didn't ask.

"Of course," Nash replied, wondering what the man would want to discuss in private. Had he found out the rest of the truth? Doubtful, but the possibility was always there.

"You're not seriously going to talk work are you?" Tessa asked.

"Not at all." Damon came to his feet and handed his plate to Linda who had just come into the dining room. "Ah, thank you. But I would've taken my own plate in."

Linda, the house cook and all around amazing lady to the family, laughed. "Of course you would've. I trained you years ago."

"Go on," Lily gestured to Damon and Nash. "I'll help clean up."

Both Tessa and Cassie both chimed in their refusal for Lily's help, but Lily stood and started gathering dishes anyway.

"I think we should pitch in, too, Ian," Grant spoke up as he scooted his chair back. "I don't know about you, but I don't want to face the wrath of my wife if I let Lily do all of this."

Reaching into the high chair, Ian pulled Emily out and tucked her firmly against his hip. "Actually, there's a smell coming from our section over here and I'm pretty sure I'm on diaper patrol. You enjoy wrapping up the leftovers, though."

Lily couldn't help but get a bit choked up at the easy way this dynamic family all meshed together so beautifully. What would it be like to live here, to have that connection every day? She had her mother and they were extremely close, but Lily wondered how raising a child in LA and bouncing him or her around from film set to film set would affect the outcome of her child's life.

"Lily?"

Nash's soft tone, his easy grip on her elbow had her turning. "I'm sorry, what?"

She realized the entire room was now staring at her. Great. She'd thought they'd all scurried out, apparently not.

She'd given off the image of a professional actress when she'd been filming on set here for months, but now they were all looking at her as if she'd sprouted another head.

"I asked if you were okay." Ian stared across the table at her and seeing him holding his stepdaughter had Lily smiling and nodding.

"I'm pregnant," she blurted out.

Nash laughed. "Way to break the news, sweetheart."

Inwardly cringing, she turned to him. "Sorry. I'm botching things up here."

He took the stack of plates from her hands and kissed her cheek. "You're fine."

Lily glanced around the room to the stunned faces. Only Ian was smiling and threw her a wink and a nod of encouragement.

"It's okay," she told them with a smile as she blinked back the tears. "Nash and I are both excited about this. While we certainly weren't planning on a baby, we are thrilled."

"A son and a new grandbaby on the way all in one week?" Damon asked as he puffed out his chest and grinned. "This calls for a major celebration."

"How about Wednesday?" Cassie suggested with clasped hands and a wide smile. "That's the fourth. We could have fireworks, grill out and make a big night of it."

Lily's head was spinning as the Barrington sisters started planning, then Linda came in, heard the news and chimed right in on everything she could make, too. As she babbled on, she bustled around the table, took the plates from Nash's hand and kept right on planning without missing a beat.

The moment went from her instant onslaught of tears to a chaotic meshing of voices chattering over each other.

"I think they're excited," Nash leaned over and whispered in her ear.

Damon came around the table and settled his hand on her shoulder. "Congratulations, Lily. I'm really happy for you guys."

Lily couldn't help the lump of emotion that settled in her throat. Nash's newly minted father was already welcoming her and the baby into the family. This was everything she'd ever wanted to give her children...a sense of belonging.

"Thank you."

Nash's hand slid over the small of her back. "We want to keep this private for now," he informed his father. "Lily is taking some time off and staying with me until we figure out the best course of action. If the media gets hold of this news before we're ready..."

"I understand completely," Damon nodded. "If you need anything, let us know. Privacy is something we value here. I promise to only keep Nash a few moments in the stables and then we'll be back and we can continue this celebration."

Nash leaned down, placed a kiss on her cheek. "I'll be back in a bit," he murmured before following Damon and the other men from the room.

Lily looked up to see, Tessa, Cassie and Linda all smiling

at her. Damn it. She wished she could label her relationship with Nash because she didn't want to bond and fall in love even more with these amazing women if it wasn't going to be long-term.

Now that Nash had come clean with his family, would he want to get closer to them? Surely he wouldn't want to just pack up and follow her back to LA. But, she had a job, a life there that she couldn't ignore.

She loved her job, not so much the lack of privacy, but digging into roles and bringing emotion to the screen. She still hadn't decided whether to take the film Ian had sent her way and she had to discuss things with Nash, too.

Lily needed to know what he was thinking, what he was feeling before she fell any deeper in love with this family.

But she was afraid it was too late for that.

Thirteen

Nash entered the stables, like he had many times before, but this time Damon walked silently at his side. The fresh, familiar smell of hay and leather greeted them, while a couple of the horses peeked their heads out to see who their new visitors were.

A tug on Nash's heart irritated him. He couldn't think of this estate as home or as a place where he would be welcome once Damon found out the truth. But he truly loved these grounds, these horses.

"Man-to-man," Damon started as he moved easily down the center aisle, his cowboy boots scuffing against the concrete. "How nervous are you about this pregnancy?"

Nash laughed. "That's not at all what I thought you'd say once we got down here. But, between us, pretty nervous. Not about the baby, and I know Lily will be an amazing mother. The worry more centers around the fact I want her to have a healthy pregnancy."

Damon stopped in front of the stall that housed Don Pedro, Tessa's prizewinning horse that had helped her secure the coveted Triple Crown and put the Barrington sisters in the history books as the first females to accomplish such a feat.

"It's rough being the man in this situation." Damon rested his hand on the top of the half door. "You're used to fixing things, being in control of everything in your life. I know when Rose was pregnant with our girls, I was a nervous wreck until she delivered. But once I held that baby in my arms, I knew for certain I'd never let anyone or anything hurt them if I could prevent it at all. I'd sell my soul to the devil himself to keep my girls happy."

Be careful what you wish for.

"Lily has had a few dizzy spells and she was told to relax and take it easy to keep her blood pressure down, so right now that's all I can concentrate on." Nash reached out, sliding his hand up the stallion's velvety nose. "So, I'm sure you didn't bring me down here to talk babies."

Damon took a step back, crossed his arms over his chest and nodded. "I want to make you an offer."

Intrigued, Nash continued his slow caress of Don Pedro's soft hair. This was where that power and control came into play. No matter what Damon said, Nash had to remember that he held the upper hand, not his father. And it was how Nash chose to play his hand that would determine both of their futures and any relationship Nash hoped to have.

"Tessa and Cassie retired, as you know. Cassie has plans to open a school for physically challenged children here and Tessa will help when she's available. She and Grant have discussed moving." Damon's gaze shot straight to Nash's, held there and demanded full attention. "I've been offered an excessive amount of money for several of my horses and I've yet to take an offer."

It took every bit of willpower Nash had not to laugh. He knew all about those offers…and the fact they'd been turned down.

"I know we just discovered each other," Damon went on. "But I'd like to offer Don Pedro to you. I've thought about this since you were here the other night and I know a gift hardly makes up for missing your entire life, but you're the best groom I've ever had and this is the best horse we've ever had. I'd like you to have him."

Nash barely caught himself before his jaw dropped. Control. He had to remain in that mindset. Damon Barrington was handing over such a remarkable horse? A horse that could pull in more money than any other at this point in time?

"I never expected that," he said honestly.

Here all this time Nash had been dishing out offer after offer only to be rejected and now Damon was hand delivering the horse right to his rival. Had he admitted the paternity months ago, would Damon still have given Nash the horse once the season was over? Or had Damon just come to know Nash well enough to know he would take care of the animal like the royalty Don Pedro was?

The fact that Nash had deceived a man he'd actually come to care about weighed heavily on his heart and his conscience. This would not end well…for anybody.

"What did Tessa say?" Nash asked.

Damon waved a hand, then reached out to stroke the Thoroughbred's neck. "She was well aware we'd be selling him after the race and she's on board. I'm selling a couple, actually, if Cassie can part with them. We all get attached, but that girl is so emotionally invested it rips her heart out to let them go after she's trained them."

Nash glanced at the horse in question, one of his main motivations for coming here. The end goal was in sight, but that last shred of truth still remained wedged between Nash and all he wanted. His goals had changed somewhat, but he still wanted Don Pedro. He just didn't know that he was comfortable using deceit to achieve that end anymore.

"I'm sure you could get a great deal of money for him from other owners who want to breed him," Nash said after a moment. "Are you sure you just want to give him away?"

"I could sell him, sure, but racing was never about money to me." Damon stepped away from the stall and crossed the aisle to show some affection to a horse named Oliver. "I had a passion for riding when I was a young boy. My mother was single and couldn't afford to give me a horse, so I would take lessons at a local horse farm in exchange for working in the barns. It was hard work, but I learned the love of the sport and saved every single penny I ever received because I was going to buy my very own horse."

A slice of guilt slashed right through Nash's heart. Hearing Damon talk of his childhood, wondering how much more their lives mirrored each other, Nash turned to face his father.

"I know hard work," Damon continued, resting his elbow on the edge of the door. "I know it pays off and I want to reward you for all you've done here in a short time. I realize you came here to technically spy on us, but I have to admit, I would've done the same had I been in your shoes."

That damn lump of remorse settled in his throat, making it nearly impossible to swallow. Nash had never expected to have a bonding moment with Damon and he sure as hell hadn't thought he'd nearly get choked up over it. But here Damon was sharing a part of his past, proving why Nash should take the free gesture of love.

Damn it.

Nash glanced back to the coveted stallion in question. Could he seriously go through with this? Just take the prize-winning horse and move on? Everything he'd wanted was right within his reach; all he had to do was grab hold.

What would Damon say once he learned the truth? Deceiving the man was initially the plan, but, now that Nash had actually spent time here and gotten to know this family, he cared for them in a way he never would've imagined.

Turning down this gesture, however, would require an explanation Nash wasn't quite ready to disclose yet. So he tightened the web he'd woven around himself and turned back to Damon.

"I'll take good care of him," Nash said with a smile that didn't quite come from his heart.

Damon's shoulders relaxed as his lips curved into a grin. "Anything for my only son."

The guilt knife twisted deeper, leaving Nash more vulnerable than he'd ever thought possible. He'd officially become the man he never wanted to be. Because in the end, he would tear apart the relationships he'd just started to build, relationships he realized he wanted more than anything.

He hadn't even known how much he longed for a family until he came here. Then when he'd discovered the baby another layer of need was added. So here he was, his heart overflowing with family bonds and relationships and in one second that all could be wiped right back out of his life.

Right now, he had to figure out a way to reveal the truth in the least damning way because that tight fist he'd had gripping all he wanted was slowly coming apart and he could feel the control slipping from his grasp.

Lily didn't remember laughing so hard in such a long time. Having an impromptu girls' day was beyond fun and quite a departure from the cattiness of the women in LA. Lily really didn't have good girlfriends back home and being here with Cassie, Tessa and Linda almost felt as good as being with her own mother.

"So what do you think for desserts?" Linda asked, crossing her leg over her knee and propping her notepad up on her thigh. "So far I only have the main course. What's your favorite dessert, Lily?"

"She's a fan of chocolate."

Lily jerked her head toward the doorway where Nash stood looking all scrumptious in his black T-shirt pulling taut across his wide shoulders and those well-worn faded jeans hugging narrow hips. His gaze zeroed right in on hers.

"I believe chocolate milk is high on the list," he added, his tone dripping in sex. "Ice cream will do in a pinch. Right, Lily?"

Lily suppressed a shudder. The man knew exactly how

to turn her on in a room full of people without so much as stepping into her breathing space.

"Why don't we do sundaes?" Linda asked, oblivious to the sexual tension.

Cassie laughed. "Emily will love that."

"I'm always up for anything chocolate, too," Tessa chimed in, pushing her hair back over her shoulder.

Lily smiled, excited to be pulled into the Barrington family like she belonged there. "Sounds like a great night. What can I bring?"

"Yourself." Cassie leaned over and patted Lily's leg. "Linda gets offended if we try to bring anything to a party she's throwing. And we've learned she's the best and anything we make won't compete so we just let her have at it. Bring Nash and an appetite. That's all."

Lily glanced to Linda who was rigorously jotting down notes, her lips thinned, her eyes narrowed. This woman was all business when it came to meal planning. Lily knew from being on the set that Linda loved to feed a houseful of people and she was an amazing chef.

"Sounds good to me," Lily said around a yawn. "Sorry, I'm so tired lately."

"It's the first trimester," Cassie told her with a soft smile. "You'll regain some energy soon."

Nash came to stand in front of her and extended his hand. "Why don't I get you home? It is getting late."

Glancing out the window, Lily realized the sun had all but set. They'd been there most of the day and time had flown by.

She took his hand and came to her feet. "This was so fun. Thanks for having us over."

"You're welcome here anytime," Tessa told her. "Feel free to come any time Nash is working. We can always use another female around here."

"Good thing the guys aren't nearby to hear that," Linda said as she rested her pad and pen on the coffee table. "But, I agree. Come by anytime."

After saying their goodbyes, Lily and Nash headed home.

Home. Had she really started thinking in terms of his house as her own? She'd spent the majority of the day being welcomed into his newfound family, she was having his baby and her feelings for him were growing stronger every single day.

Yeah, she was starting to feel as if this was home. LA seemed so far away, as if a lifetime had passed since she'd been in her spacious condo. Just the thought of going back to the lonely space depressed her. She'd never fallen in love with a place—or the people—she'd visited on location before like she had at Stony Ridge. Part of her never wanted to leave, the other part had to be realistic and see that she couldn't stay forever. Her job didn't allow her to set roots.

So how could she raise a baby with a man who lived here? How could she leave the man she'd fallen for in such a short time?

Tears pricking her eyes, that tickle in her nose and clogging of her throat had become all too familiar sensations lately. Her hormones were raging all over the place, just like everything she'd read said they would. She sniffed, turning to glance out the window so Nash wouldn't see her sniveling like some crazy, unstable woman...which she was, but still.

"Hey." He reached across the truck console and gripped her hand, giving a reassuring squeeze. "You all right?"

Lily glanced over, catching his quick look her way before he concentrated back on the two-lane country road. "I love it here," she found herself saying. "I mean, it's so nice, so laid-back. And today I felt like a normal person."

Nash's soft chuckle filled the cab. "Sweetheart, you're going to have to clarify that last part."

Staring down at their joined hands, his so large and tan and hers so delicate and pale, she tried to find the right words to make him understand.

"I'm always treated like a celebrity everywhere I go," she began. "I don't mind the pictures, the autographs, that's all fine and comes with my job. But that's just it. I do a job and that's what it is to me. I don't see myself as someone on a level above anyone else. Today everyone treated me like I was just a family friend, they welcomed me into their home and I had a fun time without worrying about work or the pettiness that comes along with the industry."

Nash continued to drive, not saying a word, and Lily started to feel a bit silly.

"I'm sorry," she finally said. "That all probably sounds ridiculous. I'm already worried about the media hounding me when I return to LA. They hover all over, even going through my garbage to get any morsel of gossip they can sell. I have no clue how to resolve that unless I do what you mentioned and make an announcement during a live interview. But this town, these people are so amazing. I'm comfortable here and it's just going to be hard to leave."

There. She'd said it. She really wanted to know how he felt on the matter and it was past time they discussed where they were headed. She was kind of glad her rambling led them down the path to a topic they'd danced around for over a week. The uncertainty of her immediate future was starting to really cause more anxiety than she should be dealing with.

"Do you want to stay?"

That low tone of his produced the loaded question she'd been asking herself.

"I want to know what you want."

Such a coward's answer, but she needed to know where he stood, needed to know what was on his mind because up until now they'd only talked seriously about his past and they'd had amazing sex. That was all well and good…better than good, actually, but there was so much more to be brought out in the open.

"I want you to be happy." He gripped the wheel tighter with one hand and continued to hold hers with the other as he maneuvered the truck around a series of *S* curves. "I want our baby to be healthy and I want us to build on what we've started."

"And what have we started?" she prompted.

She wanted him to label their relationship. Okay, maybe that sounded immature of her, but baby or no baby, she found herself wanting to be part of his world, wanting to see what the long-term outlook could be for them.

Nash turned onto his road, then into his drive before he pulled to a stop, killed the engine and turned to face her. The porch light cast a soft glow into the cab of the truck and his bright eyes seemed to shine amidst those dark, thick lashes.

"You want me to lay everything out for you?" he asked, grabbing her other hand and holding on as if his life depended on this moment. "I want you to figure out what makes you happy. Do you want to go back to LA and have the baby? Do you want to stay here until the baby is born and then see what happens? I'm not asking you to choose between the baby and your career, I'd never do that. But whatever you decide, you better make damn sure I'm part of that plan because I want this, us, a family. I'm going to take what I want and I'm not backing down."

Nash tugged her forward and claimed her mouth like a man starving for affection and staking his claim. With their hands tightly secure in her lap, Lily opened for him, relieved that he'd declared how he wanted to be with her and a bit aroused at the demanding way he'd all but marked her as his own.

Nash and his powerful mannerisms never failed to make her feel wanted and—dare she say—loved.

But she just realized she hadn't brought up the job opportunity Ian had presented her with. She had until tomorrow night to give him an answer.

When Nash eased back and looked her in the eyes, Lily knew she had an important decision to make. And this time her career move would affect the man she'd fallen in love with.

Fourteen

Lily had changed for bed, washed her face and pulled her hair back into a low, messy bun. She hadn't seen or heard a peep out of Nash since they got home. He'd come in, tossed his keys on the entryway table and told her he'd be back inside in a bit.

That was over an hour ago. She'd given him space, but what was bothering him right now? He'd been so open in the truck, then it was as though he waged some inner war with himself and he shut her out…again.

Was he having doubts about what he'd revealed to her in the car? Was he still caught up in the whole Barrington saga? Perhaps he was worried about the baby. Or maybe it was whatever Damon had discussed with Nash in the stables. Nash hadn't even mentioned the man-to-man talk and she wondered if she should ask about it or just let him decide if he wanted to open up.

Whatever had him closing her out right now, she wished he'd let her in. He only opened up to discuss his superficial emotions, but when it came to his fears Nash was a private man.

Well, too bad. If they were going to try to make this work, they needed to have an open line of communication at all times. The best of relationships struggled sometimes and they already had so many strikes against them. She refused to let go of the one man who made her feel like love was a great possibility and there was a chance for a happily-ever-after.

Wearing only her simple short blue tank-style gown, Lily padded through the house and slid open the patio door. Thanks to the light above the door she could make out Nash sitting out in the yard on a cushioned chaise lounge beneath a large old oak tree.

The warm summer evening breeze slid over her bare skin and for the briefest of moments she considered going back inside and allowing him the privacy he seemed to want. She didn't want to be that nagging woman who was always trying to get her man to open up. Even though Lily ached for Nash to talk to her, she hoped he would do so on his own.

Before she could make a move, Nash glanced her way. Even in the dim light, she saw the angst in those stormy eyes. The man held so much inside, all that worry he could be sharing with her. She knew he didn't want to upset her and he wanted her to be completely relaxed. But, how could she relax when she was constantly struggling with her own emotions and wondering what was on his mind that seemed to always put that worried look on his face?

Without a word, Nash extended his hand in a silent invitation for her to join him. Stepping from the warm, smooth concrete into the cool, soft grass tickled Lily's toes as she made her way through the yard.

When she slid her hand into his, he maneuvered her around until she sat on his lap, her legs over his thighs and her feet brushing the top of the grass. Her head fell against his shoulder, a move she'd become so comfortable with.

Nash's deep breathing combined with the crickets chirping in the distance had Lily smiling at another layer of the simple life she absolutely loved. Relaxing here would be no problem at all. And raising a child in this calming atmosphere would be a dream. Perhaps she could live here. Why not? Who said she had to live in LA? She was well-known, her agent shopped scripts for her and she would have to go on location regardless of where she lived.

When Ian scheduled her live interview, she could confess her pregnancy, open up about the man she'd developed a serious relationship with and explain they are keeping things private and had purposely kept away from the limelight.

Could the solution be so easy? So within her reach?

"Sorry I disturbed you," she told him, breaking the silence. "I started getting worried when you didn't come back inside."

Nash's arms tightened around her waist. "I lose track of time when I sit out here."

"I can see why." Lily trailed her fingertips along his tanned, muscular forearm. "So quiet and peaceful."

He flattened his palm against her belly, spreading his fingers wide. "How's our girl?"

"Safe and healthy."

He turned his head slightly to kiss her forehead. "And you? How are you feeling?"

"Hopeful," she answered honestly.

The rhythm of his heartbeat against her shoulder nearly matched hers. There was so much going on inside her, so many unanswered questions, but there was something she had no question about.

"I love you," she whispered into the darkness. His body tensed beneath hers. "I know we've really gone about everything backward and I don't expect you to say anything back. But I have to be honest with you because I need you to know how serious I am here."

When he remained silent a little piece of her heart crumbled. While she didn't expect him to return her feelings, she'd had a thread of hope that he would. She wanted to know how deep he was in with her, but he continued to be a man of mystery, because she never could get a good grasp on exactly how he felt.

Oh, he'd said he wanted to be with her, but that didn't necessarily mean love. And she so wanted a family, a real family. She didn't want to settle for less…and she *wouldn't* settle for less.

When the silence became too much to bear, Lily started to push off Nash's lap, but those strong arms around her tightened. "Don't go."

On a sigh, she closed her eyes and leaned back.

"You're everything, Lily," he said after a minute had passed. "I had no idea what my life had been missing until you came into it. But I'm still working through some things, still struggling with my identity."

The fact that she was worried about herself had guilt coursing through her. Nash had a great deal of life's obstacles thrown at him all at once.

"I want to give myself to you completely." His hands covered hers over her stomach as his soft, raw words washed over her. "I want nothing to come between us. This baby we've made is a blessing and I'm not taking our little family for granted. I just need some time to come to grips with everything and get things in order for us."

Easing up, Lily turned in his arms. Tears flooded her eyes. "Oh, Nash. There's nothing you need to get ready for us. I'm sorry I put you on the spot, but I couldn't keep the truth from you any longer. I think I started falling in love with you the moment you first swept me up into that loft."

Cupping her cheek with one of his rough, calloused hands, Nash's eyes zeroed in on hers. "I don't deserve you."

"You deserve everything you've ever wanted," she retorted with a smile as a tear slid down her cheek.

With the pad of his thumb, he swiped the moisture away. "I hope I get it."

Lily laid a kiss on his lips before shifting to lie against him once more. "Am I hurting you?"

"Never."

He may not have been able to give her the words she wanted to hear, but she knew he loved her. All those demons he battled internally kept him from speaking the truth, but Lily knew in her heart that Nash was in love with her.

"I have a film opportunity," she told him. "I think it's a good choice."

His body stilled beneath hers. "Are you going back to LA?"

Lacing her fingers through his, she settled their hands in her lap. "Not yet, but I will have to for a bit if I take the role. I would actually do the entire film there. I also still need to go see my mom, too."

"What's the role?"

Lily laughed. "Something I've never done before, actually. It's an animation and I'm pretty excited about the prospect because I think this will be a really big hit."

Nash stroked his thumb across the back of her hand. "And what does Ian suggest?"

"He said it's perfect, especially since I can record in a studio and not worry about my growing tummy." Lily turned her head to look up at Nash. "But I wanted to discuss this with you before I gave him my answer."

Piercing blue eyes met hers. "When does he need an answer by?"

"Tomorrow night."

Lily's heartbeat quickened. She'd never discussed her career with anyone other than her agent before. Never had anyone else to consider when making a film choice. This new territory was interesting and slightly nerve-racking.

"Do you want to take the role?"

"I think I do."

Nash shifted in the chair, causing her to sit up and look down into his eyes.

"What would you do if you weren't pregnant and you

didn't know me?" he asked, sliding his hand over her bare thigh.

"I'd take the role."

With a squeeze to her leg and a sexy, rugged smile, Nash nodded. "Then that's what you should do. I don't expect you to recalculate your life, Lily. You still need to do what makes you happy."

A weight she didn't know she was carrying was lifted off her shoulders. "Ian said recording wouldn't start for a couple months, but he's getting me the script to look over. Aiden O'Neil is going to play opposite me."

"Wasn't he the guy in one of the scripts you just turned down?"

Lily nodded. "He declined after he heard I wouldn't do it. He's a good friend, like Max. And this will be a good change of pace for me. Hey, no hair and makeup, either."

Nash laughed. "You're stunning no matter what you have on." Those eyes darted down to her lips as his fingers trailed up her thigh and beneath the cotton gown. "Or don't have on."

The man could get her body to respond with the simplest words or lightest of touches.

"You know you're the only man I've let get this close to me since the scandal." She trembled as his hand continued to glide over her skin. "I never thought I'd get this close to someone again, let my heart be exposed to the chance of being ripped apart."

Nash's looked at her seriously. "You humble me, Lily."

"If you want to try to make this work, you're not going to be able to avoid the media. Not once the pregnancy is out there."

The muscle in Nash's jaw ticked. She knew he didn't want to be thrust into the public eye. Resting her hand against the side of his face, rubbing her thumb along his bottom lip, Lily leaned in and whispered, "Take me inside and make love to me."

In one swift move, he had her lifted and turned to straddle his lap. Then his hands were lifting her gown to her waist. Lily leaned forward and clutched his shoulders as he worked the zipper on his jeans.

"Or not," she added as he threw her a crooked grin.

"I don't want to wait," he said, easing a hand between her legs to stroke her until she thought her eyes would roll back in her head. "Do you?"

Lily shivered, holding on tight to him so she didn't fall. "No," she whispered as he continued to torture her. "Please, Nash."

She'd come out here wearing a flimsy nightgown, sans underwear and she thought he could wait to get inside the house? Hell no. Nash wanted her here, now.

He also wanted to not discuss how the media would hone in on them. The last thing he needed was being identified before he could fully disclose the rest of his life.

The little moans escaping her, the way her hips rocked against his hand and seeing her eyes closed, head tilted back as he pleasured her was nearly his undoing. Not to mention the perfect distraction for both of them.

Damn it, he owed her so much…a debt he could never repay because while she was freely handing out her love, he was still betraying her by keeping a lie bottled inside.

The thought of having her walk out of his life once she learned the truth would be the equivalent of taking a knife to his heart. Because he loved her. God help him, he did. And when she'd whispered those sweet words to him, it had taken all of his willpower to remain silent.

He couldn't tell her he loved her, not when there was such a heavy lie that still hovered between them. He could only show her how much she meant to him. Once he revealed himself, after he'd talked with Damon one more time, Nash would truly open up and tell her every single thing she deserved to know.

Nash removed his hand, gripped her hips and eased her down onto him. Making love to Lily with the warm summer breeze embracing them like lovers, Nash wrapped his arms around her and tugged her toward him, capturing her mouth. Her fingers slid into his hair, sending him another reminder that he was living a lie. The longer hair, the scruffy beard, the rental home…all of it was a lie.

All of it, except for the fact he loved her, loved this baby and wanted a lifetime with them both.

As her body started to tremble, Nash felt himself losing control. She broke the kiss, looked him in the eyes, just like when they'd been in his hallway.

Those dark eyes held his as her body tensed. "I love you," she told him as her body broke.

And as Nash followed her over the edge, he wished he could repeat those words back to her.

The food had been amazing and now the entire Barrington clan was gathered on the back lawn, waiting for the fireworks show that Damon had no doubt shelled out a pretty penny for, considering they'd planned this impromptu party very last-minute. But when a man had his financial padding, he could afford to snap fingers and plan such niceties with little notice.

Blankets were lying side by side and some front to back creating the effect of an oversize outdoor carpet. Ian, Cassie and little Emily sat on one blanket. Another quilt had Grant and Tessa all snuggled together. Lily was nestled between Nash's legs, her back leaning against his chest. And surprisingly Damon and Linda were on a quilt together, laughing and…whispering?

Was something going on there?

Nash smiled. Good for Damon if he was seeking happiness. He'd been without his wife for so many years, concentrating on raising his family and climbing to the top of the horse racing industry.

Nash rested a hand on Lily's stomach. He would do the same thing for his child. Nash wanted to give his baby, and Lily, everything they deserved and more.

She'd already made plans to visit her mother this coming weekend. Nash figured while she was gone, he could have a heart-to-heart with Damon and come clean with him.

He kept telling himself he was waiting on the right opportunity. No other time would work to his benefit except while Lily was gone. He could only hurt so many people at a time without crumbling himself. And he had to remain strong or he'd never be able to fight to keep what was his.

When the first spark and boom lit up the sky, Emily squealed and jumped to her feet. "Look! Look!"

Nash watched the adorable toddler with bouncing blond curls. Her infectious laughter had everyone watching her reaction as opposed to the show in the sky.

"She is precious," Lily said.

Cassie grinned. "Thanks. I was afraid the noise would scare her, but obviously not."

With each colorful burst, Emily clapped or jumped up and down. Nash caught Tessa's glance to Grant, a smile tugged at her lips and Grant's hand came around to her stomach, as well.

Interesting. Looked as though they had their own announcement to make.

Yeah, he needed to finish revealing his identity sooner rather than later because he wanted to be part of this family with no lies hovering between them. If they would accept him after all was said and done. He also had to have a long talk with his mother. Lily wasn't the only one who needed to share news about her pregnancy. Nash hadn't wanted to tell his mom over the phone, either.

"I'm going to grab a bottle of water." Lily came to her feet and looked down to him. "Want anything?"

A do-over? A chance to make this all right from the beginning? A lifetime to make it up to her?

"I'm good," he told her. "I would've gotten your water for you."

Lily laughed. "I'm perfectly capable of getting my own water."

As she moved around him, he saw Tessa hop to her feet as well and head in Lily's direction. Within seconds, Cassie and Linda followed.

Emily settled onto Ian's lap and Damon turned toward the others. "Looks like our ladies have deserted us."

The fireworks continued, the thunderous sound filling the warm night.

"I'd say Tessa is telling our news," Grant replied with a wide grin.

"She told me this afternoon," Damon said, his smile matching Grant's.

Ian's head bounced back and forth between the two men. "Well? Do I get to know what's going on?"

"We're having a baby, too," Grant said.

Ian leaned over and slapped Grant on the shoulder. "That's awesome, man. Congratulations."

Nash nodded in agreement. "I'm happy for you guys."

"I'm sure they're all back there chatting about babies and pregnancies," Damon said, leaning back on his hands. "Linda has treated my girls like her own since Rose passed. I'm sure she's all over Tessa, asking about her eating habits and if she's resting enough."

"Oh, I'm making sure of it," Grant supplied. He raked a hand through his hair and sighed. "But her emotions are all over the place."

"Dude, they're not going to settle down anytime soon," Nash informed him. "Lily can go from crying to laughing in seconds."

Ian smoothed Emily's curls down, as they kept blowing in the wind. "Cassie has been wanting another baby," he said. "I'm sure all this baby talk will only speed up the process. We'd discussed waiting another year."

"My family is growing." Damon beamed, glancing up when Linda came back and settled down next to him. "These are exciting times."

"Indeed they are," Linda said as she patted Damon's leg.

Oh, yeah. Something was definitely going on there.

Cassie, Tessa and Lily came back and took their seats. Lily clutched her water bottle and leaned back against him.

Nash leaned over and patted Tessa on the arm. "Congrats on the baby."

Tessa lit up, just like Lily did when they discussed their baby. "Thanks. I'm so excited."

Chatter ensued as the fireworks came to an end. An hour later they were all still discussing babies, due dates, baby showers and growing families. Emily had long since fallen asleep in Ian's arms and Nash felt a tug on his heart. He couldn't wait to cradle his own child to sleep, to know that he was a comfort and security for someone.

Lily tipped her head, kissed him slightly on the lips. "Thank you for bringing me here."

"I didn't bring you," he replied, hugging her tighter against him. "Your movie brought you here."

She ran her hand along his arm. "You know what I mean. You've included me in your life, in your new family even though we're still new ourselves. I feel like I belong here, like I belong with you. You don't know how much that means to me."

Yeah, he did. He knew she valued family just as much as he did. He knew she wanted their baby to have that special bond.

But would Nash sever that bond once he revealed himself?

Nash kissed the end of her nose and squeezed her tight again. "You deserve this."

And he just had to find a way to convince her he wasn't purposely deceiving her and that she belonged there. She belonged with him.

Fifteen

Taking the first step in getting his life back under control was long overdue. He loved Lily. There was no denying the fact anymore. Now with her in Arizona visiting her mother, he was at the Barrington estate about to confront his father and put one hell of a kink in their newfound relationship.

He should've let this out earlier, but he'd just not been ready. Since falling so hard for Lily, Nash knew putting it off any longer would be an even bigger mistake. Starting now, he was going to set things straight and take control of his life.

Here all this time he'd thought he'd been in control. He'd only been controlled by his own lies and selfishness.

Nash paced the living room. He'd already gone into the kitchen and said hi to Linda, who was washing up dishes from breakfast. She'd invited him to stick around for lunch, but Nash didn't make any promises. He highly doubted he'd be welcome at that point.

Nerves curled deep in his gut and a vulnerability he hated to admit he had threatened to consume him. But he wouldn't back down. He wouldn't take the coward's way out.

"Nash, I was surprised to hear from you today." Damon crossed the room and Nash came to his feet. "Not that you aren't welcome anytime. What brings you here on a Saturday morning? Is Lily with you?"

Nash shook his head. "She went to visit her mother in Arizona. I needed to talk to you about something important."

Damon laughed and smacked his hand on Nash's shoulder. "Last time you said that you announced you were my son. What else could you have to tell me?"

Raking a hand through his long hair, hair that he couldn't wait to cut off so he could get back to looking like himself, Nash gestured toward the chair. "You may want to have a seat."

Damon's smile faltered. "Is something wrong with your mother?"

"No, no. She's fine." Nash sank to the sofa, resting his elbows on his knees. "I actually drove down to see her yesterday after Lily's plane took off. She's excited about the baby."

Nervous chitchat would only postpone the inevitable for so long. He'd come here on a mission and he refused to let nerves take over.

"I actually came to tell you that I can't accept Don Pedro from you."

Damon's silver brows drew in as he eased forward in the leather chair. "If you're concerned about the money I could make by selling him, don't be."

Shaking his head, Nash clenched his fists. Damn it, he hated this. "I know you're not concerned with the money. I know this because I've been offering to buy him for nearly three months now."

Confusion settled onto Damon's face as the elderly man drew his brows together in confusion. "I'm not following you."

"You've been getting phone calls from Barry Stallings."

Damon's back straightened. "How do you know this?"

Holding firm to his courage, Nash leveled Damon's gaze. "Because Barry is my assistant."

Damon stared, studied for a minute, then gasped as realization dawned on him. Jerking to his feet, he started shaking his head.

"How can this be?" he whispered, as if to himself. "You—you're…what the hell game have you been playing? The long hair, the beard. You're a bigger man than I remember. Then again I haven't seen you in person in years. How long have you been planning to come here and spy on me? Was the son angle just a convenient reason? Or are you even my son?"

For once in his life, Nash remained seated, wanting Damon to feel in control. Nash had never relinquished power to anyone before, and certainly not to his longtime rival, but right now, rivalry was gone and this was about so much more.

"I haven't lied about the fact I'm your son," Nash began. "I did find out when my mother had a stroke several months ago."

"Jake Roycroft is my son." Damon's jaw clenched. "So, you came in deceiving us from day one with this fake name, long hair and a beard. Your clothes are all worn and even your truck is dated. You sure as hell thought this betrayal out down to the last detail."

There was no other angle to look at it. Damon was dead-on.

"I did," Nash confessed. "I wanted to come in, find out what you had planned for your horses after retirement. I needed a prizewinner to breed with mine and I wanted the best.

"Finding out I was your son was like a slap in the face," he went on, putting everything on the line for the family he'd come to love…the rival he always thought he'd hate. "I couldn't believe it. But my mother's gut-wrenching confession was all the proof I needed. She'd kept the truth from me, from you, because she knew it would tear us up. She'd watched this feud for years, but when she had her stroke, she couldn't keep the secret anymore."

"And what was your plan when you first arrived?" Damon

asked, his tone anything but that of a loving father or the cheerful man who'd walked into this room moments ago.

Now Nash did rise. He needed to pace, needed to get out of here, but he had to stay and continue to unravel this damn web he'd caught himself in.

"I was hoping if I got a good idea of what your plans were for the horses, I could get my assistant to offer enough money to take them."

Nash crossed to the mantel where a new photo of Tessa, Cassie and Damon sat. The trio stood in front of Don Pedro after the historic win of the Triple Crown. Nash hadn't been there, he'd been here at Stony Ridge taking care of the other horses.

Other photos showed Rose holding her two young daughters in front of a waterfall, a teen Tessa atop a Thoroughbred, Cassie in a ring with another horse. The family was tight and Nash wondered if he'd ever truly be able to break in where he longed to be.

"I was also battling whether or not to tell you the truth about being your son." Nash turned back around. Damon hadn't moved, except to cross his arms over his chest. "But the more I got to know you all, the more I learned as the film was being shot, I realized you weren't the enemy I knew over the years. You were a ruthless businessman to me, but with your family…you were a different person."

Nash refused to succumb to those damn emotions that he was nearly choking on. He wouldn't show weakness, not now. Remaining strong was the only way he would get through this.

"Between sneaking around with Lily and battling how to tell you who I was, I was torn. I decided to tell you everything after the film crew left, after Lily and I were finished and after you'd hopefully sold the horse to my assistant."

Damon's eyes narrowed. "That all changed when Lily became pregnant. Right?"

Nash nodded, disgusted by the look of hatred he'd put in Damon's eyes.

Being cut off from the Barringtons would kill Nash, but he would take it like a man. He'd done all of this to himself and had nowhere else to place the blame. Every downfall that was about to happen was nothing less than what he deserved. Nash just prayed the people he'd come to care about had mercy on him.

"Have you been lying all this time to Lily?" Damon asked.

The man may as well have punched him in the gut. Nash rested his hands on his hips, glanced away and nodded.

"So she knows you're my son, but she has no clue you're a millionaire with your own estate, your own spread of horses," Damon repeated as if to drive that knife deeper. "She thinks she's fallen in love with a simple, hardworking, honest groom. You waited until she left town to confront me and, what, you expect this to all be tidied up for when she returns?"

Damn it, why did that explanation make Nash sound more like a bastard than a man who'd started off with good intentions?

"I'm telling her everything when she comes back," Nash replied, forcing himself to hold Damon's angry gaze. "I love her. I didn't come into this expecting to get wrapped up personally with anybody at all, least of all Lily. Then our affair started and spiraled out of control. Then I got to know you all even more and I started wanting more than what I came here for. I started out with a goal to get Don Pedro at any cost. Now, though, I don't want him. I just want Lily, I want my father. You have all the power. You can cut me out of your life or we can try to make this relationship work."

Damon continued to stare through that narrow gaze.

"I understand if you don't want anything to do with me." Nash had laid it all out there, had even offered a meager defense. Now he had to finish up and get the hell out before he started sobbing like some damn fool. "I wouldn't blame you for cutting me out of your life. I mean, I haven't been part of your life for very long, so you could just go back to the way things were before I ever came around. Nothing would change for you, really."

Linda stepped into the doorway. "Damon—"

"Not now, Linda."

She moved farther into the room until she was standing beside Damon. "Don't make a decision you'll regret later."

Nash jerked his attention to the elderly woman who was gripping a kitchen towel in her hands, her knuckles white. He'd never guessed he'd have an ally in any of this, but having anybody at all on his side was a blessing he didn't deserve.

"Linda, you don't know what you're talking about," Damon said between clenched teeth. "This is between me and Nash. Damn it. Jake."

"Nash is my real middle name," he replied, as if that made any of this easier to swallow.

Linda laid a hand on Damon's arm. "I know you're hurt, but if you'll put your pride aside for two minutes, you'll see he's hurt, too. And, he's still your son. That's something he never had to reveal."

Damon's eyes flashed toward Nash's. Odd, now that everyone had been calling him Nash for months, he'd come to think of himself as Nash, the groom, as opposed to Jake, the billionaire.

"I don't want to make this harder for you," he explained. "I wanted to get everything out and I did. I'll go and leave the next step up to you."

Leaving with so much hurt between them, leaving with so many questions still left unanswered would kill him. But Damon needed to come to grips with this just as Nash had. Realizing his rival was also his father had taken Nash months to digest and he couldn't expect Damon to do so in the span of a few minutes.

Silence filled the room as Damon continued to stare at

Nash in disbelief. Linda still clutched the towel as her eyes darted back and forth between the two stubborn men.

"You know how to reach me." Nash raked a hand over his jaw, the beard he'd become so familiar with bristling beneath his palm. "I won't contact you again."

Damon said nothing as Nash headed toward the foyer, but there was one last thing his father needed to know. One last bit of his heart he'd lay on the line, even though he would surely damn himself later for being so open and vulnerable.

Gripping the door frame, Nash turned to look at his father for what would probably be the last time. "For what it's worth, I enjoyed the past several months. I'd wondered about my father my entire life and even though I was shocked that it turned out to be you, I wouldn't trade my time here with you and the girls for anything."

Those threatening emotions choked him as Nash headed out the door, leaving Stony Ridge and his father behind.

That part was over, and as hellish and gut-wrenching as it had been, Nash knew what had transpired between his father and himself was absolutely nothing compared to the hurt and the anguish that awaited him when Lily returned. The thought of causing her pain was killing him.

She deserved to know the truth once and for all. And he deserved nothing less than watching her walk away. Now he had to figure out a way to keep the inevitable from happening.

Sixteen

Being away from Nash for a week had been harder than she'd thought. She'd loved seeing her mother again, but she truly missed the man she'd fallen in love with. Lily found herself missing the Barringtons, as well.

In the two weeks she'd been gone her little belly had pooched out just enough to have her smiling and gliding her hand over the swollen area. Not a drastic change to anyone looking at her, but she noticed and she had no doubt Nash would notice. That man knew her body better than she did.

She'd been careful not to wear anything tight, plus she donned sunglasses and a hat when traveling through the airport. The last thing she wanted was anyone finding out about the baby before she could make an announcement.

Nash's idea of her dropping the bomb before the media could speculate was brilliant. With the Barrington film getting buzz already months before release, Ian already booked her a one-on-one interview with a popular TV anchor. And perhaps by then she'd have some other news to share...maybe even a ring on her finger. Dare she hope that Nash was ready to follow her confession with one of his own?

Lily had changed her flight to a day earlier. She hadn't been able to wait to get back to Nash, to have him see how her belly and their baby had grown. She wanted his hands on her, wanted to share this moment, silly as that may sound.

Lily had rented a car at the airport, eager to surprise Nash since he thought he'd be picking her up the following morning. As she pulled up next to his old truck in the drive, she smiled and killed the engine.

The porch swing swayed in the breeze, as did the hanging ferns. This cozy home was perfect for their family. Images of her lavish condo in LA flashed through her mind and Lily knew that second that she didn't want her child growing up in a town with so much chaos. This porch would be the perfect play area for a toddler, the wide drive would serve as the place where their child could ride a bike or make chalk drawings. The expansive backyard just begged for a swing set complete with slide and maybe a sandbox.

When Lily looked at this house, she didn't see it as Nash's home anymore, she saw it as their future. Even though he was just renting it, she had fallen in love with it and wanted to stay. Perhaps if she offered the owner a fair price he'd sell to them.

One goal at a time, she promised herself as she stepped from the car. A light drizzle had accompanied her drive in and now the rain started falling a bit harder, faster as she made her way to the front door. The luggage in the car could wait. Her need to see Nash couldn't.

The front door was unlocked, such was life in the country, and another reason she wanted to raise her family there.

As soon as she stepped over the threshold, she smelled that familiar, masculine scent that could only be associated with the man she'd fallen in love with. She'd missed that smell, missed the feel of his body next to hers as she slept, missed the way he would hold her, look at her, bring her a random grilled cheese when she hadn't even said she was hungry.

And her body ached to touch him again. She'd gone so

long without sex before meeting Nash, but since that first time with him, she constantly craved more. Nash was it for her.

No longer did she fear the media and what they would say. They'd talk regardless and half the "news" was made up stories anyway. No, she knew Nash would be by her side; he wouldn't let her go through any of this alone. She was that confident in their newfound relationship. They'd come so far from the frenzied affair in the loft. Even their passion had reached another level of intimacy.

"Nash," she called as she stepped into the living room and clicked on a lamp. Dusk was settling outside and the promise of a storm was thick in the air. "I'm home."

Footsteps from the back of the house had her turning toward the hall. The sight of him shocked her, leaving her frozen in her place and utterly speechless.

The sight of him wearing only a pair of worn jeans riding low on his hips and nothing else but excellent muscle tone was enough to have her go silent and just enjoy the view. But, it was the clean-shaven face and the new haircut that had her doing a double take.

Those piercing blue eyes surrounded by thick, dark lashes were even more prominent now. His hair was wet as if he'd just gotten out of the shower. He froze, resting his hands on his hips. Apparently he was just as surprised to see her as she was about his transformation.

"You're early," he stated, brows drawn in. "Is something wrong?"

"Everything's fine." Lily took a step forward, then another until she'd closed the gap between them. Reaching up to cup his face with both hands, she studied this new Nash. "Why the change?"

Not that he looked bad. The Nash with the beard and unkempt hair was rugged and mysterious. This Nash with the square jaw and chiseled cheeks, with more emphasis on those mesmerizing eyes was flat-out sexy and intriguing.

"I needed to," he told her, taking her hands in his. He

kissed her palms before placing her hands on his chest. "It's the first step in getting where I need to be, where we need to be."

Lily couldn't stop taking in the sight of him. Who knew a dark beard and disheveled hair could change someone's appearance so much?

Those worry lines between his brows had deepened and the haunted look in his eyes hadn't been there when she'd left.

"Something's wrong." The feel of his quickened heartbeat beneath her hand confirmed her suspicions. "Talk to me."

Releasing her hands, he slid his own around her waist and pulled her against him. When he froze and jerked his gaze down, Lily smiled.

"I grew a little," she explained, lifting her oversize T-shirt to expose her slightly rounded belly. "One morning I just woke up and there it was."

She wondered how he'd react to her new shape, but when both of his hands came around to cover the swell, Lily knew he was just as excited about their growing baby as she was.

Nash dropped to his knees, laying his forehead against her stomach as his thumbs stroked her bare skin. The thought that this child could already bring such a strong man to his knees was so sexy.

Lily threaded her fingers through his much shorter hair. "I've missed you so much," she whispered.

The first rumble of thunder shook the house, rain pelted the windows harder now. Nash glanced up at her, a storm of his own flashing through his expressive eyes as he came back to his feet and gathered her against him.

He tilted his face against her neck, his lips tickling her skin and sending jolts of need streaming through her…as if she needed any more encouragement to want this man.

"I've needed this," he murmured. "Needed you."

Lily wrapped her arms around his bare waist. "You'll always have me, Nash. I'm in this forever, but you keep holding back. When will you open up and let me in? Finally see that what we have only gets stronger each day?"

Nash pulled back, and lightning flashed through the window, illuminating his handsome, yet troubled face. "I've always known how strong we are, Lily. I've never doubted it, never once thought what we had wasn't real. I didn't want to admit it at first because I knew you'd be leaving and I was going to have to say goodbye, so I was protecting myself. But you mattered to me the second I made you mine up in that loft."

Her body trembled at the memory even though she had a sinking feeling there was more to what he had to say.

"You're right, I've been holding back." He stepped away, raking a hand down his smooth jaw. "I never intended for you to get caught in this war I made with myself. I figured once you were gone and we parted ways you'd never have to know."

Chills crept up her spine. What was he about to confess? Was he married? Did he already have children somewhere? Was he dying? The endless questions swirled around in her head until she thought she'd pass out.

Gripping the back of the sofa, Lily met his gaze head-on. She wasn't about to cower now. Whatever he was on the verge of telling her obviously was tearing him up, too. If they were going to be a couple, they needed to face the crisis together.

"You said that about Damon being your father," she told him. "Is there another secret you've kept from me?"

"I need you to know I never meant for you to be affected by this."

Wrapping her arms around herself to ward off the tremors overtaking her body, Lily held her ground. She didn't move, didn't blink. Whatever this was, it was bad.

"You also need to know that I love you," he continued. "I fell in love with you before you told me about the baby. I've wanted to tell you, wanted you to know."

When he stepped forward and reached for her, Lily took a step back, holding her arms out to her side. "Don't. Don't preface whatever bomb you're about to drop with love and think that will fix this. You're picking an awfully convenient time to express the feelings I've tried to get you to share for a while now."

Nash nodded, drawing in a shaky breath. "You're right. You deserve more than what I've given. Just promise you'll hear me out before you make any decisions regarding us, our baby."

"Just tell me!" she yelled, fear spawning her outcry.

The lights flickered, but came right back on as thunder and lightning filled the night. How apropos for everything that was taking place inside this house, inside her heart.

"My real name is Jacob Nash Roycroft. I'm known as Jake to nearly everybody." He took a deep breath and let it out. "I'm not a groom, I'm a horse owner myself. All of this was a setup to spy on Damon."

Air left Lily's lungs as she stared at the man who was quickly becoming a stranger right before her eyes. "Why?" she whispered.

"Damon Barrington has been my rival for a couple of years now." Nash glanced down, raking a hand over his head before he lifted his tormented eyes to meet hers again. "We both own racehorses and I knew he and his girls were retiring. I wanted to go undercover so I could see how to get some of his prizewinning horses because he wouldn't sell them to me. I also wanted to see him as a man outside of the business world. I didn't even know going in if I would tell him about being his son. Every single day I battled this and before I knew it, we were in an affair and by then I was in too deep."

Everything he told her weighed heavily on her heart. He'd lied to her from the beginning. He had his own horse farm, he was a racehorse mogul.

Which meant he had money. Plenty of money and he

was used to getting his way. Which would explain his take-charge attitude, his beautifully appointed home, the doctor who made house calls, no doubt because Nash had paid her a hefty sum.

There was no way to describe the level of hurt that spread through her, leaving her cold, empty. Everything she'd known…no, everything she'd felt had been a lie based on nothing but a man who was only looking out for himself. Anything she felt was for a man who didn't even exist…except in her heart.

"You bastard," she whispered, hugging her midsection. She refused to look at him, she wouldn't give him the satisfaction of seeing her broken.

"My name may be different and my bank account bigger than you thought." Nash's bare feet shuffled across the hardwood floor as he came closer. "But I'm still me, Lily. I'm still the man who wants to be with you. I'm still the man who fathered that child."

His palm cupped her chin, lifting her face so she had no choice but to look him in the eyes. "I'm still the man who loves you."

There was no way to stop the tears from spilling over. She didn't even try. She hadn't wanted him to see her vulnerable, but she'd quickly changed her mind. He deserved to see the results of his lies, his betrayal. He deserved to hurt just as much as she was hurting. If he loved her so much, then she'd hate to see how he treated his enemies.

Swatting his hand away, Lily pushed off the back of the couch and stood straight up. "Don't touch me. Never touch me again. You don't love me, you love yourself. I don't think you're capable of loving me, Nash…or whatever the hell your name is."

She'd thought being deceived years ago had been bad, but this was a whole new level of crippling pain.

She'd take public humiliation any day over having her heart shattered into so many pieces she feared she'd never

find all the shards. She'd been so sure she could trust him
with everything.

"Hear me out."

"No." There was no way she would listen to more lies.
"I'm done here. You had ample time to tell me the truth, but
you started everything off with a lie."

Her heart ached and she feared the cracks and voids would
never be filled.

"You want to know what's worse?" she asked, her words
wretched out on a sob. "I still love you. Damn you, I can't
just turn off my feelings. I can't be cold to someone I care
about and I never thought you'd be so heartless to me. How
dare you make me feel again, make me think I could trust
you after you know what I've been through? How dare you
make me love, make me believe in a family I've wanted for
so long?"

Nash's eyes shimmered and Lily had to steel herself from
feeling any pity. She had no room in her heart for him...not
anymore.

"Please, Lily." He started to reach for her again, but as
soon as her eyes darted to his hand, he dropped it. "I'll do
anything to make this right. Anything so you can see how
I've changed since we started seeing each other. You need
to know that you are the reason I changed, the reason I told
everyone the truth. I did it all because I love you. I want to
be with you with nothing between us. Tell me what I can
do, I'll do it."

Even hearing him pour his heart out, bare his soul, Lily
couldn't trust that what he said was true. How could she?
For months he'd found it so easy to lie. Not only to lie, but
to sleep with her, make a baby and pretty much set up playing house, all while lying straight to her face.

He was used to getting what he wanted and now that she
was done, he was pulling out all the pretty words he thought
she wanted to hear. Nothing could fix what he'd done, what
he'd destroyed.

"I can't be here."

She pushed him out of the way and headed toward the foyer. She'd just scooped the keys to her rental up off the entry table and placed her hand on the knob when Nash, Jake…whatever, placed his hands on either side of her head and caged her against the door.

The warmth of his chest against her back had her sucking in her breath. Damn her body for responding to his nearness. Her heart was broken, but her hormones hadn't received that message.

"We can work this out," he whispered in her ear. "I can't lose you."

Lightning illuminated the sky, the electric flickered, once, twice. Darkness enveloped them, the silence mocked them. There was a time they would have made use of this raging storm, the power outage. Right now, though, they were strangers, back to square one. Because she definitely didn't know this man standing so close to her she could feel the breath on her cheek.

Being deceived once in a lifetime was enough, but this was the second man to lie to her face and make a complete fool out of her. And even though this time had been just the two of them, the pain and anguish was beyond intensified compared to the first time.

"Let me go," she whispered as her throat clogged with more tears. "Just…let me go."

One hand came around, cupping her stomach and Lily choked back a sob. "Never," he rasped, nuzzling her neck with his lips. "I'll never let go of my family. I'll give you space, I'll do anything you ask me to. But not that. I love you too much."

Lily shook her head, circled his wrist and eased his hand away. "You don't understand," she said, turning to face him, his mouth just a breath away from hers. "This is one thing you can't buy back. You can't control or manipulate with money or power. You're dealing with real people, real feelings. I hope you were able to get those horses you wanted to so damn bad."

She jerked on the door handle behind her, causing his hand to fall away. "And I hope losing me and this baby was worth it."

"You can't go out in that storm."

Lily laughed as the sudden wind whipped her hair around her face. "I'd rather face this storm than stay one more second with a man who thought he could keep my heart in one hand and his secrets in the other."

Jake stood on the balcony of his master suite looking out over the land on his estate. He'd sneaked into his own home after midnight as the raging storm died down. He couldn't stay in the rental cottage another second. Every room smelled like Lily, held memories of their passion. The few bottles and potions of hers she hadn't packed for her trip dominated the vanity space in the bathroom, her small clothes hung next to his in the closet and she'd left a pair of sandals by the back door.

He had nowhere else to go but home…a place he'd always wanted her, but where she would never be. The rain had reduced down to a drizzle, but he didn't care. He felt nothing. Not the cool rain, not the emptiness in his heart, not even a yearning to go to his own stables and look things over since he'd been gone for months.

There was nothing left for him now. On a mission to see his father, gain prizewinning horses and not hurt Lily, Jake had managed to damage everything he'd set out to obtain.

Money wouldn't buy his way out of this because Lily was right, he was dealing with people's feelings and all he'd done was trample all over them in his quest to be number one.

Droplets of rain ran down his smooth face and Jake swiped the moisture away as he turned to go back into his bedroom. The second-floor master suite was impressive in size, but that damn king-size bed dominating the middle of the floor mocked him. Sleeping alone would be hell. Knowing he'd never reach for her again, feel her curvy body against his or her soft breath as she slept…at least if she had her way about it.

But he hasn't been lying when he'd said he would give her space. He'd do whatever it took to get his family back. He knew she'd be hurt from the truth, he didn't blame her. He just didn't know how gut-wrenching seeing her emotional breakdown would be.

Jake jerked off his clothes and shoved them into the hamper in the corner of his room before heading on into the open shower. He couldn't sleep, wasn't even going to attempt it.

As he stood amidst all of the showerheads pelting him with scalding water, Jake wondered how much time Lily would take. He would give her space, but he'd be damned if he'd let her go without a fight and there was no way in hell he'd ever let his child go.

Jake flattened his palms against the tile wall, dropping his head as the water pulsed against his neck. He had a fight ahead of him, a fight he'd never had to take on before. Business, horse racing and training, that's what he knew.

What he didn't know was how to fix all the broken hearts he'd left scattered all over his life.

Seventeen

Lily felt like an absolute fool. When she'd left Jake's home three days ago, she'd not been thinking of anything but how to get away from him. There was only one place she could think of to go and here she sat in the Barringtons' kitchen, sipping orange juice and wondering what in the world she should do next.

"Honey, you're going to have to eat something," Linda said.

The woman had been an absolute comfort these past couple days. She'd not asked questions, she'd merely opened the home up and Damon had even told Lily she could stay as long as she needed.

Problem was, she needed support, comfort, a shoulder to cry on and she didn't want to admit it. But they had fussed over her; even Tessa and Cassie had come over to comfort Lily. They'd brought some clothes when they found out she'd left his house with nothing but the suitcase that had still been in the trunk of her car.

To be coddled and pampered wasn't why she had come, but she had to admit, nursing wounds with people who weren't going to stab you in the back was a refreshing change

from her LA life. She could stay there—okay hide there—
until she figured out what to do.

Today, though, her doctor was coming by the estate to
give her a checkup. Since leaving Jake's house, she hadn't
been feeling well. Of course, she'd not been eating a whole
lot, either. She made herself eat for the baby, but in reality
she probably needed more.

Insomnia had become an unwelcome friend, too. She was
in a strange bed, alone and heartbroken, but she'd keep that
to herself. The last thing she wanted was pity from anybody.
All she wanted was to make sure her baby was healthy and
then she needed to confront Jake. As much as seeing him
again would kill her, she needed to discuss the baby. He was
the father and there was nothing she could do to change that
cold, hard fact.

"Maybe just some toast," Lily told Linda, trying to avoid
eye contact with the caring woman.

"After the doctor leaves, I expect you to eat a full lunch."
Linda put a piece of toast into the toaster and turned back
around. "No excuses. You need your strength for that baby
and to fight that stubborn man of yours."

"He's not my man."

Linda laughed. "Oh, honey. Of course he is. He made
some major mistakes, but you love him. You just need time
and so does he. He should suffer for what he's done, I agree
with you there, but don't make any major decisions right
now."

Lily took another drink and smiled. "I couldn't agree
more about the suffering, but I don't think time will make
this hurt any less. He lied to me, Linda. Twice. I can't forgive that."

The toast popped up just as Damon entered the kitchen.
The man looked about as rough as Lily felt. His silver hair
was a bit disheveled, the dark circles beneath his bright eyes
proved he wasn't getting sleep.

Join the club.

"Sit down," Linda ordered. "I want to talk to you, too."

Damon jerked his gaze toward her, but Linda wasn't looking at his shocked expression as she was lathering a generous amount of butter onto the thick slice of toast.

The older man remained standing, crossing his arms over his chest. "Say what you want to say so I can get out to the stables."

As calm as you please, Linda crossed to Damon, pointing her finger in his face. "You are being pigheaded. I know Jake hurt you, that's understandable. However, have you thought about what you would've done in his situation? Would you have opened up to your greatest rival and bared your soul? No. You would've treated it like a business move. You would've been just as calculating and secretive."

Guilt churned in Lily's stomach. So many people were hurting all because Jake felt he'd had no other choice.

"Maybe I would've." Damon nodded slightly. "But we're not talking about me." His attention turned to Lily. "What about her? What excuse does he have for deceiving her?"

Linda's eyes softened as she took a slight step back from Damon. "She was an innocent bystander who got caught up in the family drama. Jake loves her, I've seen how he looks at her."

Linda smiled, resting her hand on Damon's cheek. "Just as he's come to care for you and all of us. He's hurting, too, Damon. Can't you reach out to him? See if there's any way you can work on this relationship? He's your son. You can't forget that."

Lily cupped her stomach with both hands, wanting this nightmare to be over, wanting to go back in time and make Jake open up to her. But he hadn't trusted her enough to let her in. Hadn't trusted what they had together to share his life in full.

"Why are you so hell-bent on being in Jake's corner?" Damon asked.

With a slight shrug, Linda moved to take Lily's now-

empty glass and put it in the sink. "I'm on the outside looking in. I can see people I care about in pain and I don't like
it. This family is too close and life is short. You above all
people should know that."

Lily winced as Damon's shoulders fell, and he blinked his
eyes as if trying to gain control of his own emotions. Linda
had gone straight to the heart with that veiled hint at Rose's
unexpected death.

The doorbell rang before anyone else could say a word.
Lily was all too eager to step away from this emotional battle
because beneath all of this chaos, Linda and Damon shared
something much deeper than the standard employer-em-
ployee bond.

"That will be the doctor," Lily said as she escaped. "I'll
get it."

Lily was anxious to see how the baby had progressed,
eager to hear that sweet heartbeat that made the whole world
seem perfect and right. She had to focus on her child right
now. Her love life, or the love she'd falsely believed in, would
have to wait because this innocent child came before lies,
deceit and broken hearts.

Entering the open wrought-iron gate flanked by stone
pillars, Lily steered her rental car into the long drive lined
by pristine white fencing.

She couldn't believe she was actually there. Nerves had
her hands shaking as she maneuvered up the drive toward the
impressive two-story colonial-style home. White columns
extended up from the porch, stabilizing a second-story balcony that stretched across the house. A separate three-car
garage sat just behind the house, and off to the left of the
drive were the massive white-and-green stables.

Horses out in the field swished away flies as their tails
swiped back and forth. An old oak dominated the front yard,
but the tire swing dangling from a sturdy branch caught her

attention. Why would Jake have a tire swing on a tree? He was single and didn't have any children…yet.

The landscaping around the wide porch had to have been professionally done with the perfectly placed variegated greenery and pops of color from various buds.

She should have turned around. The house was too inviting and the last thing she needed was to be drawn into this part of Jake's world.

As easy as it would be for her to convince herself to turn around, she had things to discuss with him. They were bound forever, whether she liked it or not, and the doctor had expressed some minor concerns with the baby. Jake deserved to know. Unfortunately, she needed his help, too. As much as she hated to admit it, she couldn't impose on the Barringtons any longer. She'd been there nearly a week and, after her appointment, she knew she needed to stand strong and take control back in her life.

Lily stepped out into the summer heat and made her way up onto the wide porch. Colorful pots filled with various greenery decorating each side of the door made for a picturesque entry. Everything about Jake's home looked like something out of a magazine.

This was not what she'd expected at all. Jake's rental house had seemed homey, but that had been a stage, a prop in his game. His real home was just as inviting, if not more so.

Lily rang the bell before she could change her mind and race back to her car. Moments later a young lady, probably somewhere in her early thirties, answered the door. The beautiful woman with long, blond hair had eyes the color of emeralds and a pleasant smile. Jealousy punched Lily straight in the gut.

"Hello," the lady greeted. "Can I help you?"

Whoever this woman was…

No. Lily had left Jake, so what he was doing now was none of her business. But seeing that he'd moved on so fast only intensified the hurt she'd lived with for the past several days. Or had this woman always been here waiting on Jake?

"Wait...aren't you Lily Beaumont?"

Celebrity status strikes again. "I am," she replied, trying to find fault with the stranger, but her beauty was flawless. "Is Jake here?"

The young woman nodded with a smile. "He's down in the stables," she said, pointing across the way. "He won't mind if you go on down. He told us you may stop by."

Anger slid through her veins, gliding right through the hurt he'd caused. "Oh, he did, did he?" she asked, raising a brow. "Thank you."

Turning on her heel, Lily's sandals slapped against the concrete as she marched her way toward the stables. The heat was nearly unbearable and Lily had to focus on the open doorway to the stable. Once she had her say, she could get back in her air-conditioned car and cool down, then this wave of dizziness would subside.

Of course, trying to keep her blood pressure down was a bit difficult at the moment. How dare Jake alert...whoever that lady was that Lily would be coming by? What a cocky, ego-inflated—

The rant died a quick death in her mind when she stepped through the open door and found Jake shirtless, holey jeans riding low, sweat glistening over every bare spot her eyes took in as he cleaned out one of the stalls.

He hadn't seen her yet, which gave her the opportunity to appreciate the beauty of his body. Just because she was pissed at him for lying didn't mean she was dead. Jake had the sexiest body she'd ever laid eyes on...which is how she ended up in this predicament to begin with. Saying no to a man like Jake was impossible.

Stepping farther into the stables, she stopped halfway up the aisle and crossed her arms. "Don't you have a staff to do this for you?"

Jake jerked around, bumbling with the pitchfork in one

hand before he caught it with the other. Gripping the top of the handle, his eyes drank her in, his chest heaving from obvious exertion. Lily had to remember she was here for one reason only…and it wasn't to appreciate the beautiful male form standing before her.

"What are you doing here?" he asked.

Holding her ground, Lily shifted her stance. "Why are you acting surprised? Didn't you tell the pretty blonde that there was a possibility I'd come by?"

Damn it, she hadn't been able to hold back that stab of jealousy in her tone, and from his amused smirk he'd picked up on her green-eyed monster, too.

"She's my maid," he informed her, swiping his forearm across his forehead.

Lily rolled her eyes. "I don't care what she is. What you do in your time now isn't my business."

Silence settled between them until a horse shifted in its stall. She hated the uncomfortable cloud that seemed to hang over them.

"You do care," he told her, dropping the pitchfork into the stall. "You wouldn't be here if you didn't."

Oh, that ego she once found attractive was so damn maddening right now.

Tilting her chin and taking a step forward, because Lily knew who really held the power here, she stopped only a few feet from him and cursed herself when her eyes dropped to that sweaty, chiseled chest. She couldn't hold on to her control if she was being tempted by the devil himself.

"Actually I'm here because I just had a checkup." Lacing her fingers just below her stomach, Lily held his gaze. "She said my blood pressure is still high and I need to start taking precautions to keep it down. There's some concern with me and the baby, so she said she wants to see me again in two weeks instead of the usual four to make sure the condition is under control."

"Damn it." He raked a hand through his damp hair,

rubbed the back of his neck and met her gaze. "What can I do? I know I've caused you more stress, that can't be helping. Tell me what I can do to fix this."

The worry etched over his face almost moved her. But that worry was for the baby.

"Actually I'm not here to get help from you," she said. "I'm here to ask what you paid the doctor to care for me. I'm reimbursing you."

"Like hell you are." Jake closed the gap between them, the tips of his boots nearly touching her bare toes. Those bright eyes were now blazing, the muscle in his jaw clenching. "You're not paying me a dime. This is my baby, too."

"I had a feeling you'd say that," she muttered as a wave of dizziness swept through her. Lily closed her eyes for just a moment, waiting for it to pass before she opened and met his still-angry gaze. "So I'm at least paying half."

"I pay for what's mine," he all but growled. "I will take care of my family, no matter what the needs are. It's best you realize that now."

Black dots danced before her and Lily shook her head, wiping the sweat from the back of her neck. "Could I get some water?"

In an instant Jake's hands were on her shoulders, touching her face, brushing her hair back. His eyes instantly held concern and worry. "Are you dizzy?"

Damning herself for showing weakness the one time in her life she needed to be the strongest, Lily could only simply close her eyes and nod.

Before she knew what was happening, Jake had swept her up into his arms and was carrying her out of the stables.

"Don't," she protested, but even to her own ears the plea sounded feeble. "I just need water. I'll be fine."

Ignoring her completely, Jake reached the back door to his house and squatted down far enough to turn the knob. Once inside where the cool air-conditioning hit her, Lily was already feeling as if the world had stopped tilting so much.

Jake closed the door with his foot and took her straight to the living area where he laid her on the oversize leather sofa.

"Jake, is everything all right?"

Lily didn't open her eyes, but she recognized the female voice from the lady who had answered the front door. Tossing her arm over her eyes, Lily wished she would've just phoned Jake instead of coming there. She'd wanted to show him she was just fine without him, wanted to prove she could get along alone.

And here she was, flat on her back, depending on him and now his girlfriend/maid was taking part in Lily's humiliation.

"Could you get a bottle of water, please, Liz?"

"Of course."

The cushion next to her dipped and Jake's hand covered her stomach, then his fingertips were at the base of her throat. She missed those hands, missed how they could go from showing strength caring for horses to dominating her body in the bedroom.

"Your pulse is out of control."

"I just got hot," she defended, ignoring her betraying hormones. "Once I get some water and sit for a minute, I'll fine."

"What have you eaten today?"

Shifting her arm to behind her head, Lily glanced up at him. "I had some orange juice and toast a couple hours ago."

His eyes narrowed. "Lily—"

"Mom said you wanted some water."

Lily jerked her attention just beyond Jake's shoulder and saw a young boy with honey-wheat hair tousled by the wind or just the lack of a comb. He came closer, extending the bottle to Jake.

"Thanks, buddy."

The boy smiled, showcasing a couple of missing teeth. "Hi," he told her. "I'm Tyler."

Lily couldn't help but smile back. The boy had no clue who she was and that was just fine with her. He was adorable, but Lily couldn't help but wonder who he was to Jake. The boy looked nothing at all like Jake, but he didn't resemble the lady he'd referred to as mom, either.

"Tyler is Liz's son," Jake informed her as if sensing where her thoughts had gone.

"Hi, Tyler. I'm Lily." She took the water from Jake and sat up a little higher as she uncapped the bottle. "Thank you very much."

"You're welcome."

He turned and ran toward the back of the house, obviously finding nothing exciting with the new arrival.

Taking a long drink, Lily welcomed the cool liquid as it slid down her throat. She needed to get out of Jake's house. The longer she stayed, the more questions she had and she really had no business asking them since she'd left Jake. Well, she physically left him. Emotionally had they ever truly been vested? When a relationship was built on lies it was really difficult to say who left whom first.

When she twisted the lid back on, Jake took the bottle and set it on the coffee table. "Lie down. I'll get you something to eat."

Remaining upright, she shook her head. "I'm not staying, Jake. I just need to pay you and I wanted to let you know about the baby and my appointment. I'll never keep secrets from you."

His shoulders fell and he gave a curt nod. "I deserved that."

Lily laughed. "Oh, Jake. You haven't begun to get what you really deserve."

"Then let me have it," he challenged, his chin tipped up now. "Say what you want, ask whatever you want. Don't shut me out, not when we have so much between us."

He was serious. He truly thought talking would place a bandage over the hurts and they'd go on their merry way to make a family and happily-ever-after. If she started on her rant of how hurt and angry she was now, she feared she'd never stop.

"Whatever we had between us was a lie," she reminded him. "No matter how much you wish you'd done things differently, you still chose not to come clean with me, with Damon. You can't claim to care about us when you hurt us so deeply."

Jake stared at her for a minute, his eyes penetrating straight to her heart. Smelling him, sitting this close to him, within reaching distance of his bare torso, was pure hell. She missed the man she knew, the groom. The man before her was a stranger, a millionaire, but still…he was the man she'd fallen in love with.

Jake jerked to his feet and walked out of the room, leaving Lily confused. He wasn't going to fight? Was he done here?

Seconds later he came back in and stood beside the sofa. "I know you hate me, I know you want nothing to do with me, but I have a proposition for you."

Lily stared up at him. "You've got to be kidding me."

He settled back down beside her, taking her hands in his. Lily tried to ignore how the simple gesture still made her heart beat faster, how she wanted to keep that familiar touch locked away forever. She wanted to tug her hands back, but she wouldn't be childish. Whatever he wanted to say, she'd hear him out. Fighting at this point was moot. The damage was done and she'd officially steeled her heart…okay, she was in the process of doing so, which was why he needed to stop touching her.

"Where have you been staying?" he asked.

"At Stony Ridge."

"I figured," he muttered. "I want you to stay here."

"I don't want to be here at all, let alone to stay."

"Give me one week," he pleaded, his eyes never leaving hers. "That's all I'm asking. One week for you to see the side of me I wasn't able to show you. After seven days if you still want nothing to do with me, I'll let you go. I will still want to be part of my baby's life, but I won't pursue you anymore. I just want you to see the man I've become, the man who loves you and wants to show you he's not the selfish bastard who originally came to Stony Ridge."

Lily needed to tell him the rest of what she'd learned at her doctor visit, but she hated admitting she needed anything from him.

When she remained silent, Jake squeezed her hands. "Don't listen to your mind, Lily," he murmured. "Listen to your heart. You even told me yourself that you couldn't turn off your feelings. I'm only asking for a week. Let me take care of you, show you how we could be with no secrets, no lies."

One week. It was a drop in the bucket compared to the time she'd already spent with him. But how would her heart be at the end of that time? Resisting him was hard on a good day and she had no doubt he'd pull everything out of his arsenal to win her back.

She just had to be smarter, stronger and remain the one in control. Jake couldn't know how much he still affected her.

"The doctor also told me I needed to stay off my feet and let others do things for me." Lily closed her eyes, sighed and refocused on Nash. "I can't keep imposing on the Barringtons. Looks like you get your wish. I'll give you one week, but that doesn't mean I'm falling back into the way we were before."

Liz chose that moment to step into the room carrying a plate and a glass. When she set them on the table, Lily laughed as Jake thanked her.

"Grilled cheese and chocolate milk?" Lily asked, quirking a brow.

"Your favorites."

Why did he have to be so damn sweet at times? This was the same man who purposely betrayed her. She had to remember that. Who's to say he wouldn't resort to those tactics again?

"You owe me nothing," Jake continued, picking up where he'd left off before Liz had come and gone. "But I'm willing to give you everything. I'm laying it all out there for you to see."

Determination poured from him; he was serious and he wasn't backing down. It's not as if he could break her heart any more than he already had, and at the end of the seven days she'd leave. She'd go back to LA or even Arizona to visit her mother and then on to the set to record the animated film she'd just signed on for.

Lily continued to hold his gaze. "I won't sleep in the same bed as you."

Jake opened his mouth, but Lily cut him off. "That's my nonnegotiable. I'm not here to play house."

His eyes darted to her lips, then back to her eyes. "Deal. But, do you really think you can be here any amount of time and not fall back into my bed?" He eased forward, laid his hands over her stomach and feathered his lips across hers. "Now who's the liar?"

Jake came to his feet, set the plate on her lap and walked out of the room. Her lips tingled from the barely there kiss and she cursed her body for the ache that spread through her, begging for more.

Only an hour into her seven-day stint. Why did she feel as though she'd just fallen right into his perfectly laid trap?

Eighteen

Lily had chosen the bedroom upstairs at the opposite end of the hall from Jake's. That was as far away as she could get.

Day one down. Only six more to go and she would be free to leave for Arizona to see her mother again before heading home to LA. The thought of going back across the country both thrilled and worried her. She was eager to get going on that animation film, but going back to all the shallow people, the chaos of daily living and the lavish lifestyles just didn't appeal to her anymore.

Last night before bed, Lily had sent off a quick text to Ian, letting him know where she was. More than likely the Barringtons knew, but she figured she should at least let her agent know what was going on.

Not that it was anybody else's business, but she didn't mind if Ian shared where she was staying. These were complicated circumstances, after all.

Lily was thankful for the adjoining bath and it would serve Jake right if she spent the rest of her seven-day term in her room. No doubt Jake would show up at her door with trays of food so she didn't have to get up. He'd take the bed rest seriously and he'd use it to his advantage—best she knew that going in. She was allowed to get up and move around, but for the most part, she was supposed to be down with her feet up.

She'd showered and changed into the dress Jake had picked out that day they had gone shopping. Damn it, he'd see this as a sign she was giving in. Little did he know most of her clothes were still back at the rental house and this dress just so happened to be in her suitcase...a suitcase he'd had Linda pack up and bring out to the estate. He was still taking control and she wasn't sure if she was warmed by the fact or ticked that he still felt he had a right to be in charge of her life.

Pulling her wet hair up into a clip, she slid on her flip-flops and made her way downstairs. Before she could hit the landing the doorbell chimed, echoing throughout the house.

When Lily hit the bottom step, she glanced through to the foyer where Damon stood, hands in his pockets and glancing around as if he was just as uncomfortable being there as she was.

Was he here to see Jake or her?

Lily remained on the steps as Jake's footsteps fell heavily on the hardwood floors.

"Damon," Jake greeted. "This is a surprise."

"I apologize for coming by so early," Damon told him. "Is there somewhere private we can talk?"

Jake nodded. "Liz is in the back making breakfast. We can go into the living room. Should I tell her to set an extra place at the table?"

Lily gripped the banister, feeling like perhaps she should slink back upstairs and not eavesdrop on this conversation. But she didn't move.

"I can't stay long," Damon replied.

Jake nodded, leading the way into the living area. Lily slid down and sat on the step, grabbing the slender post for support. Damon was here for one reason: he was either ready to forgive Jake or he was letting him go. A portion of Lily's heart broke for Jake. Even with all the lies and deceit, she worried how he would cope if he lost his father forever. Jake was a strong, determined man, but just discovering your parent and then losing him would be crushing.

"I'm not sure if I should be worried or glad that you showed up on my doorstep."

Damon let out a brief chuckle. Lily couldn't see the men now, but she imagined the elderly mogul shaking his head as she'd often seen him do when he laughed.

The silence fueled the tension. Lily's heart beat so fast, she couldn't even imagine how Jake or Damon were feeling right now.

"To be honest I'm not sure how I feel myself," Damon admitted. "Your latest bombshell really spun me around so fast I didn't know how to react. But I've had several days to think about it."

Nerves fluttering in her stomach, Lily closed her eyes and waited.

"I hate being played for a fool," Damon went on. "I hate that you were that clever and I was so blinded that I didn't see through the disguise and the act."

"Damon—"

"Hear me out."

Lily took in a deep breath sliding her arms around her swollen midsection.

"We were adversaries for so long and I know finding out I was your father was a blow you didn't see coming. Your actions were made out of fear first and foremost. But I also know you're driven to succeed. How can I fault a trait you obviously got from me?"

"I still went about this the wrong way," Jake said, his tone low. "Once I started caring for you, the girls and Lily, I should've said something immediately."

"Yes, you should've," Damon agreed. "But you didn't and what's done is done. I believe everyone should have a second chance and I believe that being without my son for over thirty years is long enough. Life is short."

More silence fell and Lily was dying to know what was happening in that room. She'd listened in long enough. As quietly as she could, Lily came to her feet and headed back up the steps. Once she'd closed herself in her room, she sank back against the door.

Damon had fully accepted Jake for who he was, obviously forgiving the lies and mistakes. Even though he didn't come out and say the words, Damon wouldn't be there if he hadn't.

Lily didn't know if she could be that forgiving. Yes, she figured eventually she'd forgive him. But forgiving him didn't necessarily mean she could let him back into her life, her heart again.

Lily had only been at Jake's estate a short time, and she struggled with her emotions for him every single moment. One second she wanted to talk to him, try to figure out if they could get beyond this hurt. The next second she wanted to leave, wanted to get away because she worried she couldn't trust her feelings.

She wished she had the right answer and prayed for a miracle to guide her to where she needed to be.

Naps while pregnant were beyond amazing. Napping was a luxury she couldn't afford when home in LA or on location filming, but here in Virginia where the pace was slower and she was ordered by her doctor to take it easy, Lily fully embraced a good afternoon rest.

Besides all of that, she was tired. Tired from the pregnancy, tired from the roller coaster ride they'd been on and utterly exhausted from worrying about the future of this child. After spending time on Jake's turf, she was mentally drained and ready to pull her hair out.

Sexually, the man frustrated her. She wanted him, no matter how much her heart still hurt. He'd given her space, he'd not touched her since that slight kiss when she'd first agreed to stay, and damn if that wasn't driving her out of her ever-loving mind.

He'd never even mentioned Damon coming by the other day. Was he keeping that to himself, as well?

As Lily came down the steps, she realized she'd slept much longer than she'd meant to. The antique grandfather clock in the corner of the living room chimed four times, echoing into the empty space.

Lily glanced around, noting the photos along the mantel of Jake with his arm around a beautiful older woman, more than likely his mother, photos of him with jockeys and horses at various winners' circles. In every photo he was smiling.

She'd thought that smile was devastating with the beard, but without it, she could fully appreciate the intrigue, the devilish attitude and the power behind the man.

Laughter and squeals sounded from the front yard and Lily moved to the wide windows, shifting the simple linen curtains aside.

The tire swing swayed back and forth, Tyler held on, his legs dangling out of the hole. And Jake was pushing him.

Lily couldn't deny how the scene clenched her heart. Jake wrapped his arms around the boy's shoulders and pulled back, pausing for a moment before giving another big send-off. The wide grin across Jake's face spoke volumes for how much the lazy evening activity delighted him.

He was going to be an amazing dad. No matter what had happened between them, Lily knew that Jake would always put his child first and be hands-on. But, she couldn't help but wonder about this unique relationship he seemed to have with his maid and her son. Another layer he'd kept from her.

The fact he'd never let her fully in was the main point in that sharp blade that had pierced her heart.

Liz suddenly appeared beside Lily. "Tyler adores him."

"The feeling seems mutual," Lily replied, watching Jake's face light up each time Tyler laughed.

"Jake has been a good influence for Tyler since my husband passed away."

Stunned, Lily turned to Liz. "I'm so sorry."

A soft grin spread across Liz's face, but she kept her gaze on her son. "It's been hard, I won't lie. My husband was a groom here for several years. When he was killed four years ago, Jake asked if I'd like to work for him. I didn't know much about horses, so he asked if I could cook and clean. I know he was just looking out for us, and I could never find a way to repay him because he didn't have to take on a widow and a young child."

Swallowing the lump of remorse, Lily turned her attention back to the front yard. So many facets made up this man. Some were bad: the lies, the betrayal. But the others were so good, so…noble, that Lily hated that he'd damaged his image just to get ahead in the horse industry. Had the breeding, the prospect of winning and generating more money been that important?

"I know it's not my business," Liz went on, shifting to face Lily. "I have no idea what's going on with the two of you, but if it matters, Jake has never brought a woman here before. I can see how much he cares for you."

"He does." She couldn't deny that, but that also didn't mean they were meant to be. "He went about showing me the wrong way, though."

Liz nodded and offered a genuine smile. "Just don't shut him down, yet. Okay? Give him a chance. He's all work and traveling to see his mom. But with you, I see a different side to him and he'd hate me if he heard me say this, but he's vulnerable where you're concerned."

Lily closed her eyes, trying to block out the honest words coming from a virtual stranger. "You care for him."

"Not in the same way you do," Liz corrected. "He and my husband were good friends and had a strong working relationship. But my husband was killed during a robbery. He'd been in the wrong place at the wrong time. Jake didn't hesitate to see to all of my and Tyler's needs. I think of Jake as a friend and a hero when I needed one."

A hero. Lily opened her eyes, her focus shifting instantly

to the man serving as a little boy's hero. A man who had faults and had hurt her so deeply she didn't know how to forgive him.

"I need to get back to cooking dinner." Liz started to walk away, but laid her hand on Lily's arm. "I just wanted to make sure you knew where I stood with Jake because he loves you. He's a powerful man, but you've brought him to his knees. You're in control here."

Liz's footsteps echoed through the room until there was nothing but silence once again, other than the ticking of the grandfather clock in the corner.

Dropping the curtain back in place, Lily went out onto the front porch. The beautiful wide porch with sturdy wooden swings at both ends just begged for a lazy, relaxing day. She took a seat, curled her feet up on the deep red cushions and propped her elbow up on the back, resting her head on her fist. The gentle sway relaxed her.

Lily continued to watch the interaction in the yard, thankful she hadn't been spotted yet. Jake had invited her to stay for a week, had wanted her to see the real man he was with no pretenses, no secrets.

She was already seeing a deeper side to the person she'd fallen in love with. But could she ever get past the fact he thought it was okay to deceive her? Who's to say the next time he wanted something he wouldn't lie to get it?

Between Damon's visit the other day and seeing Jake with Tyler, Lily found herself wanting more. She just worried they were too far gone to get back on stable ground to build anything that could match the fire they had before.

A light flutter in her stomach had her pausing, her hand cupping her belly. The odd sensation happened again and Lily knew she'd felt her baby. Their baby.

The doctor had told her the first feeling she'd get in her stomach would feel like butterflies floating around. The description was pretty accurate, considering that for just a second the shocking sensation had tickled. The movement had only lasted the briefest of moments, but enough to have her smiling.

When she glanced back up, Jake's eyes were on her, and Tyler was hopping out of the hanging tire and racing around to the back of the house. Lily's smile faltered. So much tension stretched between them, so many words that needed to be spoken, so much emotion needing to be released.

Jake made his way toward the porch, and with each step Lily's heart beat faster. He stopped in front of the swing, took her feet from the cushion and sat down, placing her legs across his lap.

"Don't," he told her just as she started to shift away. "Let's just pretend this is a normal day and we're enjoying this late afternoon breeze."

His warm hands gripped her ankles, holding them securely on his lap. She hadn't felt his touch for so long, she knew she'd missed it, but she had no idea just how much his warmth affected her.

"We're not normal people and this isn't just a normal family afternoon," she whispered, hating how true her statement was.

His fingertips trailed from her shin to the top of her foot, back and forth until she couldn't control the tremors that slid through her. That powerful, seductive touch of his would be her undoing.

Jake tipped his head just slightly, focusing those bright eyes right on her as he always had, as if he could see straight into her soul. "You always say you want to be a regular person, not the celebrity when you're off location. Relax, Lily. We're both simply going to be ourselves, nothing fake, no acting. Just Jake and Lily."

Jake and Lily. As if they were an official couple. But she didn't have the energy to argue and she would remain calm to keep her blood pressure down for their baby's sake. And she was done fighting…fighting him and fighting herself.

"I think I felt the baby move a bit ago." She hadn't thought about telling him, but the words tumbled out of her mouth before she could stop them.

Jake's eyes darted to her stomach, a wide grin spread across his face. "What did it feel like?" he asked, his hand pausing in mid-stroke over her leg.

"Like someone was inside tickling me," she explained. "It was faint. The sensations happened twice while I was sitting here watching you and Tyler."

He brought his gaze back up to hers. "How long were you watching us?"

"Long enough to know you two have a special bond."

"I love him," Jake said without hesitation. "I'd do anything for him."

Lily nodded. "Liz explained the situation. I can't imagine being a single mom."

The smack of reality hit her before she realized what she'd said. Jerking her legs off Jake's lap, she came to her feet. Crossing the wide porch, she rested her hands on the white railing at the edge of the structure.

"You won't be alone." Jake's hands slid around her waist seconds later. She hadn't even heard him get up and move toward her. "I'll never let this baby feel neglected and I'll never let you feel like you're doing it all by yourself. No matter what happens with us."

Lily dropped her head between her shoulders and sighed. "There is no 'us,' Jake," she whispered. "Letting you back in…I don't know if I could survive being hurt again."

Tears pricked her eyes behind her closed lids as his fingers splayed across her abdomen. "I'm not giving up on us, Lily," he murmured in her ear. "And I won't let you give up, either."

As much as she wanted to resist him and back up her words with actions, she found herself leaning back against his chest as a tear slipped down her cheek.

"I'm not leaning on you," she told him with a sniff. "I'm not weak and I don't need you. I'm just tired, that's all."

Rubbing her stomach with gentle motions, he kissed the side of her head. "I know, baby. I know."

Nineteen

Jake swirled the whiskey around in the glass tumbler. Staring at the amber liquid wasn't taking the edge off, but he didn't want to lose himself in the bottom of a bottle, either. Right now he needed a clear head, needed to process what the hell was going on with Lily.

Keeping his hands off of her the past few days had tested restraint he didn't even know he possessed. But being with her on the porch, witnessing such raw emotions from her had nearly broken him. The damage he'd caused her was inexcusable, yet she'd leaned on him for a moment and he'd taken that as a sign of hope. At this point, he was grasping at anything she'd throw out.

She'd eaten dinner with him, Liz and Tyler and had gone to her room afterward. He hadn't seen or heard from her all evening and it was nearly eleven. More than likely she was asleep, curled up in that four-poster bed he'd bought from an antiques dealer. The clear image of her dark hair spread all around the crisp white sheets had him clenching the glass before finally slamming it down onto his desk.

If he ever wanted a chance with her, he needed to be open about everything from his life to his emotions. He needed for her to see that he'd changed, he put her first and nothing would come between them again. He couldn't let more time pass without telling her exactly where she stood in his life.

Standing just outside her door, he pondered for a minute if he should wait until morning. She was supposed to rest, after all, but he couldn't. He'd given her space and it was time she realized just how serious he was about winning her back.

Tapping on the door with the back of his knuckles, Jake swallowed and tried to ignore his frantic heartbeat. Nerves consumed him, but being a coward now would certainly secure a future without the woman and child he loved.

The knob rattled just as the door eased open. Lily stood before him, her hair spilled over one shoulder, her eyes wide. Apparently she'd been just as restless as he had. A small light glowed from the table lamp beside her bed.

"Can I come in?" he asked. When she said nothing, he added, "I have some things I need to say."

He worried she would slam the door in his face, a definite right she had, but she opened the door a bit wider and he realized her slamming the door would've been a blessing. Now his penance was having this conversation while seeing her dressed in a silky chemise, the same one he'd slid off her body many times before.

Only this time, her belly rounded out the midsection and her full breasts threatened to come out of the lacy top.

He glanced to the unmade bed, the sheets all twisted in the middle. "I'm sorry if you were sleeping."

Lily shook her head as she sat on the edge of the bed. "I wasn't asleep."

Jake remained by the door because if he even took one more step into this room he wouldn't be able to keep from touching her. Between her tousled appearance and the inviting bed that mocked him, he seriously deserved a damn award in self-control.

But he was here to lay it all on the line. Never before had he done anything so important and so terrifying.

"Damon came by the other day," he began, shoving his

hands into the pockets of his jeans. "We've come to an agreement to work on our relationship."

Lily rested her hands next to her hips. "I know. I was coming down the stairs when he arrived. I listened for a few minutes, but came back upstairs. I'm sorry I eavesdropped. I couldn't make myself leave until I knew what he wanted."

Jake smiled. "It's okay. He said the girls were upset, but they understood my angle and they wanted to get to know their only brother. Damon actually invited me over this weekend for dinner."

Lily's smile hit on every nerve Jake had. He missed that smile, missed the light in her eyes…a light he'd diminished and was desperately trying to get back. He didn't just want that brightness back for only himself, but for her. He wanted her to be that vibrant woman he'd fallen in love with, the stunning light he'd met months ago.

"I'm really happy for you, Jake."

"He asked if you'd be joining me."

Lily's eyes widened before her gaze darted down into her lap. "I don't think that's a good idea."

"I told him I was giving you time to make your own decisions," he went on, not letting her refusal deter him from his goal. "I hadn't planned on telling you about his visit because I didn't want you to think I was trying to sway your decisions."

Her dark eyes came back up to his. "And aren't you?"

"Not by telling you his choice to give me another chance." Jake pulled his hands from his pockets, massaged the back of his neck and took a deep breath. "I've time, Lily. I told you to stay for a week and I've truly tried to keep my distance. Knowing you're here, within my reach, has been one of the hardest things I've ever faced."

"I know," she whispered.

That spark of hope he'd had earlier on the porch grew stronger at her quiet confession—apparently she'd been battling the same war. Jake took another step into the room, then another.

"Tell me you're ready to give up," he told her, damning the tears that threatened to clog his throat. "Tell me the thought of living without what we have is more appealing than fighting for us."

He didn't miss the way her fingers curled into the sheets on the edge of the bed, nor did he miss her shaky intake of breath.

Her silence was invitation enough to move closer, so close he knelt in front of her, taking her hands and holding them in her lap.

"Tell me that I've got no chance with you," he went on. "Because I won't give up on us as long as there's hope. I have to believe you're not ready to give up or you would've left here before now."

Lily's chocolate eyes filled as she bit her unpainted bottom lip. "I can't tell you that."

Relief flooded him, but he was still not in the clear.

"I know we have a lot to work through," he continued. "I know I deserve nothing, but I'm asking for everything. I want you in my life, Lily. I want us to be a family. I don't care if I have to live in LA part of the time and we can come here to get away. You call the shots here."

"I'm scared, Jake. I've never loved like this before, never been so hurt because of it."

Easing forward even more, he let her hands go and wrapped his arms around her waist as he looked up into her teary eyes. "I've never loved like this before, either. That's no excuse for hurting you the way I did, but I can swear on my life that I'll never hurt you again. I want a lifetime to love you, Lily. I want forever to be the man you deserve and the father our children deserve."

She threaded her fingers through his hair. "I'm risking everything by letting you back in."

"My heart is on the line, too," he told her. "If you walked

out again it would kill me. I love you, Lily. I know when I said it before the timing couldn't have been worse. But I love you so much I ache when you're not with me."

The smile that spread across her face had tears gliding down over her cheeks. "I love you, too, Jake."

Every bit of tension and fear left his body as he leaned his head forward, resting it against their baby. Lily's fingertips caressed the back of his neck as he breathed in her familiar scent.

"I won't keep anything from you again," he murmured as he lifted his head.

"I know. You've shown me the man you are. I want to give us another chance." She stared into his eyes, and his heart swelled with love at the light shining back. "I do have one stipulation, though."

"What's that?"

Her hands framed his face, stroked his jaw. "Maybe a little scruff? I fell in love with a rugged man who turned my insides out that first night in the loft. Maybe you could not shave for a while?"

Jake laughed. "Anything you want. Besides, I'll be too busy to shave."

"Oh, really?" Lily lifted her brows. "And what will you be doing?"

Jake's hands traveled up the silky chemise to the thin straps barely containing her breasts. "I plan on keeping you in bed for the next several days."

Her body trembled beneath his. "Well, the doctor did tell me to rest."

Sliding the straps down, he peeled the lacy material over her breasts and palmed her. "Oh, you'll rest. You can just lie there while I take very good care of you."

Lily's head fell back as she arched into his touch. "You have the best ideas."

Epilogue

The grounds were as immaculate as always. The early fall sun shining high in the sky beamed down onto the intimate ceremony. The handsome groom held the bride's hands as their smiles beamed off the other. There was nothing fancy, nothing over-the-top for this outdoor wedding. An arch covered with white buds and sprays of greenery covered the stone walkway, white rose petals sprinkled over freshly cut grass and a family surrounding the happy couple.

Reaching over, Jake took Lily's hand in his. When she sniffed and swiped at the moisture threatening to slip down her cheek, Jake squeezed her hand and leaned over.

"I love you," he whispered. The man knew just how to press on every single hormonal button she had. He palmed her rounded belly with his other hand. "I love her, too. I can't wait to make you my wife."

Lily tipped her head to rest on his shoulder as she watched the couple standing before her pronounced husband and wife by the minister.

Damon kissed his bride, sealing his bond with Linda. Only Tessa, Grant, Cassie, Emily, Ian, Jake and Lily were in attendance. The quaint family ceremony was perfect. Every detail taken care of by the Barrington sisters and

Lily. For once Linda didn't lift a finger. The younger girls had wanted her to just show up and enjoy her special day.

As everyone came to their feet, Jake pulled Lily into his arms. "I can't wait to marry you next weekend."

They'd opted to hold off on their own plans until Damon and Linda were married so everybody's focus and celebration wouldn't be torn. They'd also opted to marry just before her exclusive interview in ten days, which would reveal the pregnancy and her marriage all in one shocking swoop. At nearly seven months, Lily had more energy than ever and they'd just found out the baby was a girl...as they'd thought all along.

They'd both immediately known the name—Rose. How could they name their baby after anyone but the woman who, in a roundabout way, brought Lily to the estate?

While Lily loved how private she and Jake had been for the past several months, she was eager to introduce him to her world, to show everyone that true love existed and she'd found it.

They'd visited her mother and she and Jake had clicked perfectly. Lily couldn't be happier with how her family was growing, how she was being welcomed into the Barringtons as if she'd always been part of them. Damon had fully embraced Jake, as well. The two men were already power planning for the upcoming racing seasons. Just because the girls were retiring and gearing up to open a riding school for disabled children didn't mean Damon was ready to let go just yet. Especially with his son breeding Don Pedro. The families were truly meshing in every way.

Linda and Damon turned, moving from one family member offering hugs and smiles to another. So much happiness enveloped them. Each couple had fought through pain, through obstacles that could break most others.

With three more children in the Barrington clan taking off, Lily knew this dynasty was truly just getting started.

* * * * *

If you loved
CARRYING THE LOST HEIR'S CHILD,
pick up the rest of
THE BARRINGTON TRILOGY
from Jules Bennett

SINGLE MAN MEETS SINGLE MOM
WHEN OPPOSITES ATTRACT...

Available now from Harlequin Desire!

COMING NEXT MONTH FROM

HARLEQUIN *Desire*

Available February 3, 2015

#2353 HER FORBIDDEN COWBOY
Moonlight Beach Bachelors • by Charlene Sands
When his late wife's younger sister needs a place to heal after being jilted at the altar, country-and-western star Zane Williams offers comfort at his beachfront mansion. But when he takes her in his arms, they enter forbidden territory...

#2354 HIS LOST AND FOUND FAMILY
Texas Cattleman's Club: After the Storm
by Sarah M. Anderson
Tracking down his estranged wife to their hometown hospital, entrepreneur Jake Holt discovers she's lost her memory—and had his baby. Will their renewed love stand the test when she remembers what drove them apart?

#2355 THE BLACKSTONE HEIR
Billionaires and Babies • by Dani Wade
Mill owner Jacob Blackstone is all business; bartender KC Gatlin goes with the flow. But her baby secret is about to shake things up as these two very different people come together for their child's future...and their own.

#2356 THIRTY DAYS TO WIN HIS WIFE
Brides and Belles • by Andrea Laurence
Thinking twice after a reckless Vegas elopement, two best friends find their divorce plans derailed by a surprise pregnancy. Will a relationship trial run prove they might be perfect partners, after all?

#2357 THE TEXAN'S ROYAL M.D.
Duchess Diaries • by Merline Lovelace
When a sexy doctor from a royal bloodline saves the nephew of a Texas billionaire, she loses her heart in the process. But secrets from her past may keep her from the man she loves...

#2358 TERMS OF A TEXAS MARRIAGE
by Lauren Canan
The fine print of a hundred-year-old land lease will dictate Shea Hardin's fate: she must marry a bully or lose it all. But what happens when she falls for her fake husband...hard?

REQUEST YOUR FREE BOOKS!
2 FREE NOVELS PLUS 2 FREE GIFTS!

H HARLEQUIN®

Desire

ALWAYS POWERFUL, PASSIONATE AND PROVOCATIVE

YES! Please send me 2 FREE Harlequin Desire® novels and my 2 FREE gifts (gifts are worth about $10). After receiving them, if I don't wish to receive any more books, I can return the shipping statement marked "cancel." If I don't cancel, I will receive 6 brand-new novels every month and be billed just $4.55 per book in the U.S. or $4.99 per book in Canada. That's a savings of at least 13% off the cover price! It's quite a bargain! Shipping and handling is just 50¢ per book in the U.S. and 75¢ per book in Canada.* I understand that accepting the 2 free books and gifts places me under no obligation to buy anything. I can always return a shipment and cancel at any time. Even if I never buy another book, the two free books and gifts are mine to keep forever.

225/326 HDN F4ZC

Name _____ (PLEASE PRINT) _____

Address _____ Apt. #

City _____ State/Prov. _____ Zip/Postal Code

Signature (if under 18, a parent or guardian must sign)

Mail to the **Harlequin® Reader Service:**
IN U.S.A.: P.O. Box 1867, Buffalo, NY 14240-1867
IN CANADA: P.O. Box 609, Fort Erie, Ontario L2A 5X3

Want to try two free books from another line?
Call 1-800-873-8635 or visit www.ReaderService.com.

* Terms and prices subject to change without notice. Prices do not include applicable taxes. Sales tax applicable in N.Y. Canadian residents will be charged applicable taxes. Offer not valid in Quebec. This offer is limited to one order per household. Not valid for current subscribers to Harlequin Desire books. All orders subject to credit approval. Credit or debit balances in a customer's account(s) may be offset by any other outstanding balance owed by or to the customer. Please allow 4 to 6 weeks for delivery. Offer available while quantities last.

Your Privacy—The Harlequin® Reader Service is committed to protecting your privacy. Our Privacy Policy is available online at www.ReaderService.com or upon request from the Harlequin Reader Service.

We make a portion of our mailing list available to reputable third parties that offer products we believe may interest you. If you prefer that we not exchange your name with third parties, or if you wish to clarify or modify your communication preferences, please visit us at www.ReaderService.com/consumerchoice or write to us at Harlequin Reader Service Preference Service, P.O. Box 9062, Buffalo, NY 14269. Include your complete name and address.

HD13R

Here's a sneak peek at the next
TEXAS CATTLEMAN'S CLUB:
***AFTER THE STORM** installment,*
HIS LOST AND FOUND FAMILY
by **Sarah M. Anderson**

*Separated and on the verge of divorce, Jake Holt is
determined to confront his wife. But when he arrives
in Royal, Texas, he finds that Skye has been keeping
secrets...*

Jake had spent the past four years pointedly not caring
about what his family was doing. They'd wanted him to
put the family above his wife. Nothing had been more
important to him than Skye.

He was not staying in Royal long. Just enough to get
Skye back on her feet and figure out where they stood.

Just then, the baby made a little hiccup-sigh noise that
pulled at his heartstrings.

Jake's brother picked the baby up so smoothly that
Jake was jealous.

"Grace, honey—this is your daddy," Keaton said as he
rubbed her back. Then, to Jake, he added, "You ready?"

Not really—but Jake wasn't going to admit that to
Keaton. He tried to cradle his arms in the right way. Then
Keaton laid the baby in them.

The world seemed to tilt off its axis as Jake looked
down into his daughter's eyes. They were a pale blue—

just like her mother's. Up close now, he could see that Grace had wispy hairs on her head that were so white and fine they were almost see-through.

She didn't start bawling, which he took as a good sign. Instead, she waved her tiny hands around, so of course he had to offer her one of his fingers. When she latched on to it, he felt lost and yet *not* lost at the same time.

He was responsible for this little girl from this moment until the day he drew his last breath. The weight of it hit him so hard that if he hadn't already been sitting, his knees would have buckled.

This was his daughter. He and Skye had created this little person.

God, he wished Skye was here with him. That things between them had been different. That he'd been different.

But he couldn't change the past, not when his present—and his future—was gripping his little finger with surprising strength.

Don't miss what happens next in
HIS LOST AND FOUND FAMILY
by Sarah M. Anderson!

Available February 2015,
wherever Harlequin® Desire books and ebooks are sold.

Love the Harlequin book you just read?

Your opinion matters.

Review this book on your favorite book site, review site, blog or your own social media properties and share your opinion with other readers!

Be sure to connect with us at:
Harlequin.com/Newsletters
Facebook.com/HarlequinBooks
Twitter.com/HarlequinBooks

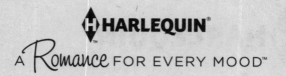

HARLEQUIN®

A Romance FOR EVERY MOOD™

**Stay up-to-date on all your
romance-reading news with the
Harlequin Shopping Guide,
featuring bestselling authors, exciting new
miniseries, books to watch and more!**

The newest issue will be delivered right to you
with our compliments! There are 4 each year.

Signing up is easy.

EMAIL

ShoppingGuide@Harlequin.ca

WRITE TO US

HARLEQUIN BOOKS
Attention: Customer Service Department
P.O. Box 9057, Buffalo, NY 14269-9057

OR PHONE

1-800-873-8635 in the United States
1-888-343-9777 in Canada

Please allow 4-6 weeks for delivery of the first issue by mail.

HSGSIGNUP

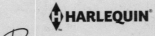